Anyone

Anyone

A Xenofreak Nation Novel

By Melissa Conway

2nd Edition published by Winged Pig Press 2020
www.melissa-conway.com

Paperback ISBN: 978-1-954352-14-8
Digital ISBN: 978-1-954352-15-5

Prologue

The closest thing to magic in this world is money.

In fiction, magic is mystical, effervescent. It uplifts the smallest and the lowest, enabling whole new vistas. In life, magic is a small plastic card that fits neatly in your wallet. I'll bet the real Cinderella's fairy godmother was loaded.

My name is Titania, after the fairy queen in Shakespeare's A Midsummer Night's Dream. My mother obviously didn't bother running a mental list of the nicknames kids could invent with a name like that. If she had, she might have spared me, especially after I sprouted early and abundantly the summer after sixth grade. Middle school was horrible enough without handing my tormentors a ready-made insult in a D-cup sling. No matter how many times I insisted my name was pronounced "TIE-tay-nee-ah," the boys would say it, "TIT-ay-nee-ah."

I am not beautiful like my namesake. I'm not even a "project" candidate—some badly-dressed, greasy-haired schlump who only needs a good scrubbing and a make-over from well-meaning popular girls in order to shine. I'd need major medical intervention to even come close, and I don't happen to have a rich godmother, fairy or otherwise, who can whisk me off to L.A. for a relaxing vacation of reconstructive surgery.

Not that L.A. is the place to go for anything anymore, unless you need some rubble. All the states along the Pacific Ring of Fire were slammed with earthquakes and volcanoes during the Cataclysm. California took the biggest hit, well, as far as loss of life and property anyway. Sure, Hawaii and Alaska are messed up, and there's a big glassy hole where Yellowstone used to be, but those places didn't lose as many people. Eastern Washington, where me and my mom used to live, got mostly burnt out. All our firefighters were off helping get San Francisco under control and there was no one left to stop the wildfires.

I had barely started my junior year in high school when the Cataclysm began. A week later, it was over and my high school, the whole city for that matter, was gone. It's been eight months, and schools all over the country are finally beginning to reopen. Everything is starting to get back to normal except in the worst areas, where martial law is still in effect. Texas took the opportunity to declare itself its own country, and for a while there, it looked like Congress was too busy elsewhere to respond. They did quash it eventually, with troops that abandoned the Middle East to the holy wars that broke out. But once communication was reestablished as power poles and cell towers were fixed, and merchandise began making its way into stores as roads and bridges were repaired, the places least affected began to get back to life as usual.

And the almighty dollar, which had been on the verge of succumbing to the brief global destruction, rebounded more quickly than anyone could have hoped. For someone like me, born poor, raised in near-poverty, it might have been nice to go to a school where the playing field had been leveled. But the separation between classes has persevered as long as there's been civilization. The rich kids have always had the advantage, even the ones who weren't born beautiful. Money is magic.

Chapter One

When it became obvious that the effects of the Cataclysm were going to uproot us from the town I grew up in, I made a color-coded map of the U.S. showing the most active earthquake faults, the locations of all the nuclear power plants in the country, and the areas prone to hurricanes, tornadoes, flood, wildfire, and extreme weather. That, plus a general rundown on violent crime by population, gave me a good idea of the places that might be safe.

Mom barely stopped throwing things into her suitcase long enough to glance at it. "We have to stay with Gramma Foster."

"In Pennsylvania? That's where Three Mile Island is!"

"And after what happened in '79, I'm sure it's been reinforced enough to withstand anything. Come on, Tainie, we have no choice. She'll be eighty this year, and we can stay for free, which is a heck of a lot better than having no house, no job, nothing."

We left soon after, only to get stuck in an endless line of cars evacuating the area. Waves of choking brown smoke preceded the fires that swept down from Canada, across the desert, fed by dry scrub brush and abandoned homes, and powered by a badly-timed Chinook wind. Luckily, mom had anticipated the need for extra gasoline. I was forced to let go of the grudge I'd been holding at only being allowed one suitcase of clothes and a small box of mementos to make room for the gas cans in our tiny Honda Civic. For the first time since my kitty Pester died, I was almost glad he wasn't around. His crate, cat box and food would have taken up so much space we might not have made it—wouldn't have if it weren't for that gasoline—like so many others trapped on America's highways in that horrible time.

I remember that first leg of our journey so vividly, but I shy away from thoughts of the terrible scenarios we witnessed as we drove past. Frightened people do desperate things. And that whole bizarre trip with Mom was frightening, so much worse than what I was feeling on the first day of school. Sure, starting at a new school was scary, but not life-or-death scary.

Gramma Foster, really my mom's step-grandmother, lived in a two-bedroom condo four blocks from Ashworth Academy. Four long blocks filled with big houses with landscaped yards, the kind of house I'd never been invited to.

It was the end of April, a bitterly cold day. The sky seemed a little bluer, but the scientists warned that the ash in the atmosphere could take years to fully dissipate. Patches of dirty snow lining the sidewalk provided safe footing from the ice. I only had the one pair of shoes; the ones I'd been wearing since the afternoon we abandoned our home—my favorite tennis shoes with the smiley-face laces—wholly unsuited for the weather.

At least I had access to Gramma's closet. The wool coat I was wearing smelled funny, but it was warm, buttoned securely across my chest, and was a heck of a lot classier than my Walmart puffy coat, which I'd left behind anyway. My feet were as big, and about as attractive for that matter, as a Hobbit's, or I'd have totally borrowed Gramma's snow boots, too. She didn't need them since she rarely left the condo.

After two blocks I had to share the sidewalk with other kids. I'd been here for months, but never met any of them. I didn't see anyone else walking alone, even though I'd been told the school district had been flooded with refugees from the west coast and trailers had been set up to accommodate all the new students.

Ahead of me, three girls dressed in fur-lined coats and cashmere scarves walked arm-in-arm. I heard laughter from behind me just before a dark-haired boy about my age wearing a brown and tan school jacket ran past. He barely avoided me by jumping into the street. A missile flew over my shoulder and nailed him in the side of the head, spattering snow in all directions.

"Oh, dude!" he yelled. I saw him glance toward the three girls as his blonde friend caught up. The girls giggled, the boys strutted, and I tried not to envy them the normalcy.

I was hoping I would get through the day without attracting any attention, but the dark-haired guy looked right into my face as he was brushing snow out of his hair. He did a classic double-take and then faced forward. He shoulder-bumped his friend as they walked, and I sensed rather than heard him alert the other boy. Sure enough, the blonde surreptitiously glanced over his shoulder at me. I met his eyes with a bland expression. I have to give them credit for trying to suppress the incredulous laughter that followed. Neither boy mocked me openly, for which I was pathetically grateful.

I looked down at my feet and stopped to retie my shoes even though they didn't need it. When I stood back up again, I tried to walk gracefully, tried to glide along like my bones weren't too big for my height, like my low brow, heavy jaw and protruding underbite were something to be proud of.

The school was a newer two-storied structure, textured grey brick and silvery reflective windows. At the center of a large round courtyard, the builders had erected a statue of a man holding an armful of books in the middle of a now-dry fountain. I wondered if water came out of his ears in the summertime. A thick gaggle of students clogged the walkway near the entrance, including the two boys who'd laughed at me, so I lingered by the fountain. A brass plaque embedded in the rim told me all I'd ever wanted to know about Ambrose P. Ashworth, founder. I read the paragraph twice, with zero comprehension.

I wanted to walk away, run away back home where I'd already gotten past the worst of the teasing and reached a point where I was accepted by most of the students. Apprehension burned in my gut like a Cataclysm volcano.

The bell rang, but I stood my ground until the only kids around were the ones running to get to class before they were tardy. I took my class schedule out of my pocket. There was no mail service; the government hadn't gotten around to reinstating it yet. Mom had gotten friendly with Mrs. Wharton, Gramma Foster's downstairs neighbor, so we could occasionally borrow their computer. We accessed the school district's website and printed my schedule from their house.

Inside the main building, despite the impression I'd gotten from the exterior that Ashworth Academy would be all opulence, the shiny green linoleum and grey-painted walls looked just like my old school. I don't know if it was the familiar smell, like musty old books buried under gym socks, or the sound of sneakers squeaking on the floor as students rushed to class, but I had the déjà vu feeling I'd been here before.

As I headed down the main hall looking for room 17A, I saw a vinyl banner strung vertically across a main intersection. I read the bold block letters with a sinking heart, if it was even possible for my heart to sink further.

The Bulldogs. What were the odds that my new school would have the same mascot name as my old? I took a deep breath and tried to pull in my jaw, tried for the millionth time to force my bottom teeth to stay behind my top, wondering how long it would be before someone suggested I be the school mascot.

First period was English, with Mr. Collins, who was, in fact,

English.

His accent immediately brought back more memories of the Cataclysm and that strange, roundabout trip to Pennsylvania. Mom and I made it out of Washington and through the mountains of Oregon and Idaho despite the landslides. She'd been driving for nearly 24-hours by the time we made it to Salt Lake City. To my surprise, she drove to the airport and parked in long-term parking. I thought we were going to sleep in the car, but she turned her normally placid face to me and said tensely, "I don't want any arguments from you. Just come along quietly for once, okay?"

I had no idea what she meant, but whenever she got that look in her eye, the fanatical gleam that reminded me of her superstitious Irish roots, I knew better than to contradict her. Besides, if her intention was to blow my meager college fund on a plane ticket that would spare me the rest of the drive, I was all for it. I had no plans to attend a place of higher learning more ambitious than the local community college anyway.

She bought two plane tickets, all right, but not to Pennsylvania.

"Open your books, class," Mr. Collins interrupted my thoughts, pronouncing the word 'class' as, "closs."

There were forty-two students in six cramped rows, all sitting with the false, polite compliance of the first day of school. Guaranteed, in two weeks, a class this size would be unmanageable, especially by the effeminate and hesitant Mr. Collins. He'd asked us to open our books, but then launched into a monologue about his qualifications, the fact that this was his first year at the school, blah, blah, blah.

I tuned him out after the first two sentences and, moving only my eyes, looked around within my field of vision. Not one of the kids sitting near me had 'potential friend' written on them. I was looking for certain signs: unattractive, physically underdeveloped, glasses—the thicker the better. The boy next to me had glasses and if I wasn't mistaken, his shirt had a Star Trek logo sewn onto the breast, but he'd blacked out his fingernails with a Sharpie and was wiggling and twitching like his ADHD meds hadn't kicked in yet.

The blonde girl on the other side of me was one of the débutantes I'd seen on the way to school. She'd draped her coat over the back of her chair, revealing three thin sweaters in varying shades of pink layered strategically over her pencil-slim body. Her heavily-mascaraed blue eyes flicked over me. I was hoping to catch a dismissive glint; instead, she looked briefly calculating, and I resignedly added her to my list of 'Girls to Avoid like the Cataclysm.'

Behind her, with his long legs stretched out under her seat, sat the dark-haired boy who'd pointed me out to his friend. I only got a quick look at his bored face, but it was enough to tell me he would be on my list of "Boys most decidedly Not to Crush on." His hair was too thick and wavy to fall properly into the shaggy seventies-style so many boys affected, so he'd had it cut shorter than was fashionable. He wasn't classically handsome; his chin was too pointed, his nose too long and his lips a little thin, but something about the way he held himself was very, very appealing. I admit I'm a sucker for unstudied confidence; probably the 'opposites attract' thing.

Mr. Collins had been droning on the whole time, but my ears picked up on his change of cadence just in time to hear the question, "How many of you have read The Iliad?"

I had, but I lowered my eyes to the contents page of my open English book. Chapter one was Grammar and Punctuation. A movement in my peripheral vision told me the dark-haired boy had raised his hand. He was the only one.

"Mister…" Mr. Collins consulted his attendance clipboard, and finished with, "Spencer. Well, you'll have a leg up on the rest of the class, then. We'll be exploring The Hero's Journey." He grabbed a stack of paper and began dividing it for the first desk in each row to pass back. "Here's the weekly syllabus. Read it, know it, do it."

I took mine and turned to hand the last sheet to the girl behind me. She didn't even meet my eyes, just took the paper, folded it and shoved it into her book. I turned back around, suppressing a hopeful grin. Coke-bottle glasses, pale skin riddled with acne, wispy, mousy brown hair. She was perfect.

Chapter Two

When the bell rang, my new best friend apparently didn't want to be tardy for her next class—even from the back of the room in an over-crowded classroom where everyone was desperate to escape, she was the first to shoot through the door. By the time I got out into the hall, she was nowhere in sight.

I shrugged, moved to stand in an inconspicuous spot against the wall and consulted my schedule. Oh, Lord, Algebra, my worst subject. It astonished me that someone capable of getting all 'A's in the majority of her classes since she'd been getting letter grades, could barely eke out a 'D' in any given Math course. I read through the rest of my classes, glad that P.E. wasn't being forced on us ever since the Surgeon General pointed out the world's poor air quality might cause havoc on growing students' lungs.

I made it through Algebra, then History and Art. Lunch was usually a social challenge, but to my utter delight, Ashworth Academy had an open campus policy, which meant the trouble-makers could go out and smoke and the cool kids wouldn't be caught dead in the cafeteria. I had a sack lunch—bologna sandwich with mayo and lettuce, a withered apple and two of Gramma Foster's 'famous,' and inedible, oatmeal raisin cookies. She put ground flax in the batter, which made them bitter, and used coconut oil instead of butter, which gave them a strange waxy aftertaste.

Not that I complained. Food was a precious commodity in many communities these days. Ironic how starvation, which had always been a problem somewhere in the world, seemed to be more under control now than it had ever been. Frantic fundraising efforts for Cataclysm relief had spread the wealth, with the end result being that both quantity and quality of food available just about anywhere had nearly equalized, for the time being at least.

Since it was the first day of school, table affiliation hadn't gelled yet. At my old school, among others, we had the Goth, Nerd/Geek, Gamer, and Stoner tables, not to mention the exalted Jock/Cheerleader table. I sat at the far end of what was destined to become the Loser table.

Across from me and two losers down, the girl with the thick glasses and wispy hair slouched over her tray, holding an open book about four inches from her face. I ate my lunch in silence, occasionally looking over at her with a friendly, come-hither openness. Her book must have been fascinating, because she didn't notice my admittedly passive attempts at initiating contact. I decided to step it up a notch and looked directly at her, wondering what she was thinking.

Quit looking at me, skank.

I jerked my gaze away, heart pounding in a sudden adrenaline rush. Had she actually said that, or had my imagination just pulled a whopper on me? I cautiously glanced at the faces nearby. Not one of them was smirking—and they would be if she'd spoken out loud. With a shaking hand, I raised the wizened apple to my mouth and bit into it.

Where had that come from?

I'd been incredibly sick not too long ago, not from the plague that hit the southwestern states or the influenza that caught the big northern cities by surprise, but with a strange illness I'd picked up in London on that ill-fated trip during the Cataclysm.

From Salt Lake City, Mom had gotten us on one of the last flights out before the airport shut down for good. We flew into New York City and from there to London. She told me we had family in the U.K. and that it was urgent we visit, but refused to elaborate. Once there, we'd rushed around the London suburbs, dodging the riots that cropped up everywhere as panicked people behaved badly in what they anticipated were their final hours.

Then in the middle of the night, mom took me on some kind of sea-going scientific vessel along with about a hundred other people. We sailed on rough water out to the middle of the North Sea. To say I got seasick is like saying the Cataclysm was a hiccup in the earth's crust. But it was after we'd returned from that strange voyage that I got so deathly ill Mom told me later she thought I was a goner. I don't remember much of it, thankfully, but ever since, weird things had been happening.

Delusional things, like the impression that I'd just read that girl's mind.

She folded down the corner of her page and closed the book. I tried one more time, offering her an actual smile. Her eyes shifted briefly my way and a fleeting look of something like disgust crossed her features. She slung her backpack over her shoulder, took her tray and left.

I studied the apple core pinched between my fingers, unoffended at Wispy's evident rejection. Behind the glasses and under the acne, she looked normal. She was probably in the throes of adolescent hormone overload. Maybe last year or the year before, she hadn't been ostracized because of the changes her hormones had thrust upon her. Maybe last year or the year before she had been, in fact, normal. Which is why she felt no affinity for someone like me; someone who'd obviously always been a freak.

Chapter Three

My last class of the day was Chemistry, with Mr. Applebee. He was a big, tall man with a round face and full red beard. He kept his brown curly hair in kind of a long pageboy, and the overall result was that of a giant out of some fairy tale. He had a genuine smile, though.

"Alright class, first things first," he said in his deep James Earl Jones voice. "You are going to partner up. I am going to call your name. Your partner will be the next person in the alphabet. There will be no negotiating. If your partner turns out to be a bully who makes you do all the work, I don't want to hear it. If your partner turns out to be lazy and makes you do all the work, I don't want to hear it. Problems with other students need to be taken up with your counselor. That's what they're here for. I am here to teach you science without blowing you up or otherwise maiming you horribly. Therefore, you will listen carefully to instructions and not deviate from them. Am I making myself clear?"

Several people mumbled, "Yeah."

"AM I MAKING MYSELF CLEAR?" Mr. Applebee rumbled.

Even I joined in and said a loud yes along with everyone else.

"Good." He lifted a sheet of paper and began reading off names, pointing to the stations the students were to occupy. Kids scrambled around, following his directions.

"Mr. Spencer," he pointed to a station at the back of the room. I knew the alphabet. My name was likely next. "Miss Strauss."

I perched on my appointed stool, not looking at my partner, the dark-haired boy from English class. He surprised me by extending his hand and saying, "I'm Fred." Not Justin or Cody or Noah, but old-fashioned, uncommon Fred.

I tried, but only managed to raise my eyes as far as his chin. I shook his hand quickly, pulling mine away before he noticed how stumpy my fingers were. "Tainie."

"Nice to meet you."

Liar. How could he act like he hadn't made fun of me? Did he think I hadn't noticed? Did he think just because I looked like a cretin that I was as stupid as one? I didn't answer, just nodded my head and settled on the stool, facing forward.

The blonde in the pink layered shirts was seated at the front of the classroom, looking back at us. Sitting next to her with a very stiff back was Wispy. If the blonde rolled her eyes any further at Fred, they'd surely disappear into her cranium.

Mr. Applebee began writing on the blackboard. "In front of each of you is a handout with the Periodic Table of Elements. By the end of this semester we will have discussed each and every element and you will be able to identify them by symbol and atomic number. You will also have a good idea of their properties and histories. Does anyone know who created the table?"

He turned from the blackboard. Once again, the only kid in class with their hand in the air was my partner, Fred.

"Mr. Spencer," Mr. Applebee's wide face held a pleased expression.

"Dmitri Mendeleev," Fred said.

"Excellent! Miss Strauss, can you tell me when Mendeleev created the table?"

I was too surprised to pretend I couldn't. "1869," I said.

"Excellent. Looks like your team is going to set the bar for the rest of the class." Mr. Applebee went back to writing on the blackboard, the chalk hitting the board with a heavy 'tink' at the start of each stroke.

Next to me, Fred grinned. I tentatively smiled back, right before I noticed he'd flipped his handbook to the page on Dmitri Mendeleev, the cheater.

Chapter Four

By the time I got 'home' to Gramma Foster's condo, I felt like the loneliest person on the planet. No one walked with me on the way; no one talked to me. I trudged past the empty, dirty bowl of the swimming pool and up the cement stairs to the second floor. Gramma's door was two down on an interior hallway with tan stucco walls covered in spider webs. She only had four small windows, two of which opened on the hallway. The builder had put in a bunch of skylights that were supposed to make up for the lack of natural light. Maintenance since the Cataclysm had been spotty, though, and the skylights were covered in ash. The resulting light inside was always dappled and gloomy, and the air was stale as old crackers.

I reached for the doorknob, but hesitated. I didn't want to talk about my day, but there was nowhere to hide in the small condo. Mom would be asleep in our allotted room, since she'd gotten a job as the night nurse to a rich paraplegic lady. But Gramma would be sitting in her lounge chair, knitting and watching her 'stories,' which were all re-runs, since Hollywood hadn't quite recovered from the earthquake damage. She'd be bored and anxious to talk my ear off.

I heard raised voices from behind the door, and it didn't sound like it was coming from Gramma's tinny old television. Inside, she was sitting on a chair at the kitchen table, flapping her hands in front of her face and saying, "It stings! Oh, Sophie, it itches!" Mom hovered behind her and kept repeating in a soothing voice, "It will wear off."

"What's wrong?" I asked.

Gramma turned to me, and I recoiled at the bright color in her cheeks. She looked like she'd fallen asleep in the sunshine, if the sun's rays could effectively penetrate the ash in the atmosphere to cause such a reaction.

"Oh, it's nothing," Mom said. "I told Edna to start taking niacin for her cholesterol, but she took a little too much."

Mom moved around from behind Gramma and said gently, "I told you only 50 milligrams at a time or you'd get side-effects." She looked over her shoulder at me and clarified, "It's harmless, really. She took 250 milligrams of niacin, which is a simple B vitamin. It won't hurt her at all, but it expands the small blood vessels for about half an hour or so and causes flushing and a hive-like reaction on the skin."

Mom was in nurse-mode with this minor emergency, so maybe I could hide out in the bedroom after all. I let my backpack, empty this morning but now full of books, slip off my shoulder. Just as I was beginning the turn to make my escape, Mom asked, "How was your day?"

I gave her an eloquent look and she murmured, "Oh, I'm sorry. Maybe tomorrow will be better?"

She was usually good about keeping the sympathy out of her voice, but I detected it, and my eyes automatically welled up. Of the two sources I could have inherited my looks from, it was clear my mother was not the culprit. I knew very little about my father, but why my normal-looking mom got together with him when he'd obviously been a complete troll, I will never know.

"Honey," she started to say, but Gramma, who'd missed the subtleties of our exchange, said, "Look at my arms!" She'd pulled her sleeves back, revealing the wrinkled, saggy skin of her forearms, mottled with pinkish welts.

"It will wear off," Mom said a little more forcefully. To me, she asked, "Do you want to talk about it?"

I averted my face so she wouldn't see the tears and muttered, "I have homework."

The bedroom was small, about ten square feet, with a full-sized daybed and a white dresser. The covers on the bed were rumpled like Mom had been sleeping when Gramma interrupted her with the little niacin faux pas. I smoothed the bedspread, knowing Mom wouldn't try to get back to sleep this late in the afternoon. Her job was within walking distance, which was perfect, since even if we hadn't abandoned the car in Utah, the gas shortage made driving a real luxury.

I hadn't lied, I really did have homework, and I was sitting cross-legged on the bed, up to my eyeballs in the Periodic Tables when she came in to dress in her uniform.

"It will get better," she said, sounding just like she had when she'd told Gramma the niacin would wear off. I braced myself for a lecture, the same one I'd gotten so many times, about how it wasn't healthy for me to be so obsessed with my appearance. About how most people in the world did not look like the super-models and actresses I saw on television. About how I should focus on my studies and find something to do in life that would make me happy. And so on and so forth until I wanted to scream.

Instead, she said, "There's pea soup for dinner, and corn on the cob from the farmer's market."

"Okay."

"I'll see you in the morning."

"Have a nice night."

She looked like she wanted to say something else, but decided against it. She dropped a kiss on top of my head and left.

Once Mom was gone, I went out and dished up dinner for myself and Gramma, who crabbed about not being able to eat corn on the cob with her false teeth. I offered to cut the kernels off onto a plate for her, but she just sniffed and said, "Never mind."

She resented us being there even though we'd taken over all of her chores and tried to stay unobtrusive. I think her resentment stemmed more from bitterness at having reached the stage in her life where independence was not an option. She had frail bones, her memory was slipping, and her heart was worn out. She was a grumpy old lady whose own children and grandchildren had forsaken her. Plus, the Cataclysm had taken her social security and the government didn't know when it would be reinstated. She needed us, but didn't have to like it.

As soon as I finished eating, I made an excuse and went into the bathroom to get ready for bed. Mom rationed everything these days, even the toothpaste, only allowing me a pea-sized squeeze. Tonight, using the excuse that I'd eaten corn, I went all out and covered the bristles of my toothbrush. I didn't look at myself in the mirror while I brushed. I knew what I looked like. My dentist back home hammered in the importance of brushing thoroughly and often, because if I didn't, my malocclusion would encourage dental decay, yadda yadda.

Well, I certainly wasn't brushing to have minty-fresh breath. Like anyone got close enough to care. I thought about the girl in the pink layered sweaters—I still didn't know her name. She had perfect teeth. They were straight and white and her dainty jaw was just where it should be.

I stopped brushing and spit into the sink, looking down at my toothbrush. I must have used too much paste after all, because my mouth felt funny, kind of tingly and strange. I rinsed it out and wiped my face on Gramma's yellow hand towel. A quick look in the mirror and—What the...? I stood there, staring at my reflection, mouth open in shock.

But it wasn't my mouth.

Chapter Five

The face in the mirror was mine. Round cheeks, broad nose, low forehead, button-brown eyes, pores that would rival the surface of the moon. My mouth and jaw, though, that belonged on a different face—the very face I'd been thinking of while brushing—Pink Sweaters Girl. My lips were now plump and red, my chin delicately pointed and my teeth were exactly the way I'd always dreamed they should be.

I turned this way and that, touching that suddenly foreign part of my face, opening and closing my jaw, baring my teeth, pulling at my skin, slapping my cheeks in confusion and fear.

"This is impossible," I said, looking desperately around the little room. I lunged for the shower curtain, pulling the cheerful sunflower-covered fabric back to see if someone was hiding in the tub, somehow playing some kind of sick joke on me. I dropped my head in my hands and stood in front of the toilet, legs shaking, mumbling, "It can't be. This is not happening. My jaw is ugly. My teeth stick out. This is not happening."

I felt that strangeness in my mouth again as I imagined my true face, only this time, my hands felt movement under them. I felt my lower jaw shift forward, my teeth crowd together and tilt at an awkward angle. When I slowly sidestepped in front of the mirror again, my face was back to normal.

For a brief, through-the-looking-glass few minutes, I'd gone completely insane.

I scuttled into the bedroom and climbed under the covers, pulling them under my chin—*my* chin—and staring into the dark. It took hours for me to finally drift to sleep.

By the time Mom came home the next morning, I'd convinced myself it hadn't happened. No matter how real it had seemed, it couldn't have happened. Maybe the pea soup was contaminated with a hallucinogenic substance, or my disappointed hopes and dreams had manifested in a perversely realistic fantasy. Whatever the cause, it hadn't really happened.

Just like I hadn't read Wispy's mind at lunch yesterday.

Walking to school was a repeat of the day before, only this morning Pink Sweaters Girl and her friends were directly behind me, while Fred and his blonde friend were half a block ahead. As a special treat, I was privy to the girls' opinions on a number of subjects, including my Chemistry partner.

"Fred's so hot."

"Yeah, but his brother's hotter."

"Of course he is! He's famous."

"I don't know about famous. Infamous maybe."

"We should take up golf."

"Yeah, I can be, like, his groupie caddie."

The girls giggled and I walked slower until they passed me and their chatter faded. The sky was dark and a light drizzle had started by the time I got to school.

In English class, I finally found out that Pink Sweaters Girl's name was Jessica and Wispy was Gina. Mr. Collins had the class break out into groups to discuss a poem. My group included Fred, Jessica, Gina and another girl named Tamika. Fred took charge by saying, "I'm Fred," and pointing at each of us until we'd given our names. It took us about ten minutes to read the poem and fill in the answers to the questions we were tasked with.

We sat with our desks facing each other, not speaking, for a few minutes afterward, waiting for Mr. Collins to direct us. He was occupied elsewhere, so Fred broke the ice with, "Where's everyone from?"

Jessica immediately reached out and shoved at his shoulder. "Here silly, you know that."

He ignored her. "Tamika?"

"Oh," said Tamika, a heavy-set girl with liquid black eyes. "We came from Arkansas."

Fred made a little *tch* sound and asked, "Little Rock?"

She nodded solemnly. We all knew that something had happened with the nuclear power plant about an hour northwest of Little Rock, but the government wouldn't say what. Everyone in the drift zone had been evacuated, though.

"Have they told you anything?" Fred tapped a pencil on his desk.

"Nope."

His eyes swung over to Gina as if he'd lost interest in Tamika's plight. "How 'bout you?"

Gina shrugged. "Tampa."

Fred's pencil tapped more rapidly and he gave a little whistle. The category five hurricane that hit Florida two weeks after the Cataclysm ended hadn't technically been considered a part of it.

Gina didn't elaborate and Fred didn't ask. His pencil stilled and he looked at me. I wondered what he was thinking behind those blank blue eyes.

You poor fugly thing.

The thought appeared in my mind, but this time I wasn't surprised. I chalked it up to my new, vividly 'improved' imagination. I opened my mouth to say, "Walla Walla," but Mr. Collins asked us to move our desks back.

At lunch, Tamika came and sat with me, which was nice since the rain kept almost everyone on campus and the cafeteria was crowded. It felt good not to be alone, even if our discussion about books we'd read was a bit stilted. She was a huge Harry Potter fan who'd segued into a huge Twilight fan, whereas I preferred more literary fiction.

"I can't believe you've never read Harry Potter," she said, taking a bite of what smelled like a peanut butter sandwich.

I shrugged and waved my own half-eaten bologna sandwich through the air. "I guess the whole magic thing just doesn't interest me." This was technically not true. 'The whole magic thing' repelled me. For as long as I could remember, my mom had been a believer in all things 'Fae.' From her colorful clothes to the fairy and dragon knickknacks cluttering our shelves to her choice in Irish folk music, Mom took her beliefs to an extreme level. It was why we'd gone to 'the Old Country' during the Cataclysm. It was why I'd almost died.

"I thought magic was universally appealing," Tamika said, her dark cheeks dimpling. I upped my estimation of her. She sounded smart and I liked smart—If only I could get her off the Harry Potter topic.

"Sure, breaking the laws of nature sounds fun," I said, "but I guess I'm too pragmatic. I prefer science over fantasy."

"Science Fiction?" Tamika asked with a hopeful lilt.

I hated to shoot her down. "No, science fact."

From behind me, a loud female voice said, "It is a science fact that the Cataclysm was caused by magic."

I widened my eyes at Tamika as Wispy – I mean Gina – appeared at the end of the table. She set her tray down and used body language to get Tamika to scootch over. Today, instead of a book, she held a mini-notebook with a purple case. After settling herself on the bench, she opened the notebook and tapped some keys. Tamika raised her eyebrows at me as the seconds ticked by and Gina didn't do anything to support her ridiculous assertion.

"This connection sucks," Gina muttered, as if that explained anything.

Finally, she turned the little notebook around for us to see the screen. “My sister goes to art school in Boston, and she told me there’s this whole movement on campus of people who believe the Cataclysm was no natural occurrence.”

I schooled my expression and leaned forward politely to look at the page. The writing was too small for me to read, but there was a head shot of a black-haired man that looked familiar.

“Who is this?” I asked.

“Before the Cataclysm started, there was this website, right? It’s been taken down now, but my sister’s boyfriend got some screen shots. The site was run by a guy who called himself Seamus the Bard…”

Gina kept on talking, but I’d tuned her out since suddenly I remembered where I’d seen the black-haired man. His name *was* Seamus.

Mom and I had been on board the scientific ship, trying to sleep on the floor of a laboratory crowded with people. Seamus came in, his black hair pulled back in a ponytail that trailed down the back of one of those long coats a pirate would wear. He began to speak, but I was too seasick to care what he was saying; something about children of the boar and the last noble and how together they would stop the Cataclysm. It was the kind of dramatic, poetic garbage my mom ate for breakfast. He stood there while the ship rolled to and fro in the storm, talking nonsense, the only other sound in the room the pathetic retches echoing out of my metal bucket.

Just before he left, he paused to say to my mom, “Thank you for bringing her.”

Through bleary eyes I saw her nod.

Gina had stopped talking. “Hello!” She waved her hand in front of my face.

“Sorry.” I shoved my half-eaten sandwich in my bag and stood abruptly. “I have to go.”

I shot Tamika an apologetic look and tried too hastily to get my legs out from between the table and the bench. The toe of my shoe snagged on the underworkings and I went down, seemingly in slow motion. Sprawled on all fours in the aisle, I expected laughter and wasn’t disappointed. It came from all around me, like stereo.

“Are you okay?” A saccharine voice from above and behind me was accompanied by not a kick exactly, but more like a nudge to the ribs with a stylish booted foot. I scrambled to my feet and looked up into Jessica’s mock-concerned face.

“Fine, thank you.”

Jessica tucked a strand of her blonde-streaked hair behind an ear as the laughter faded. Everyone in the near vicinity waited for her to say more. Like a voyeur into her mind, I knew she was trying out and rejecting scathing comments: *Have a nice trip? I've seen elephants with more grace. A simple curtsy will do*.

Before she had a chance to settle on a suitable put-down, I hurried away, arms crossed defensively. I made it out into the near-empty hallway, relieved to have gotten out of there without officially becoming Jessica's target. The longer I could avoid another confrontation, the better. I wondered which classroom I could hide out in from now on during lunch. At my old school, the art teacher let me stay in his room as long as I worked on projects for his class.

I headed in that direction.

"Hey, Tainie! Wait up." I looked around and there was Tamika and Gina, a united front marching determinedly toward me.

Chapter Six

That afternoon back at Gramma Foster's condo, Mom was already awake when I walked in and took off my coat. I wanted to ask her about my hallucination, but she was ironing one of her uniform tops and seemed angry.

"What's wrong?" I asked.

"I forgot my laundry yesterday morning and some jerk stole it right out of the dryer! Every uniform I had was in there except the one I wore last night." She gestured to the item of clothing that was getting rough treatment from her aggressively wielded iron. "Old Lady Spencer has eyes like a freaking hawk. I know she's going to notice I'm wearing the same top. Believe me when I say you do not want to give that woman ammunition to criticize."

I'd heard Mom refer to the "old lady" before. This was not the paraplegic woman she'd been hired to care for, but her mother, a battle-axe of a woman who had little patience for the hired help. Mom's uniform tops all looked alike, so if the old lady could tell them apart, she must be formidable indeed.

Then something occurred to me. "Old Lady Spencer?"

Mom set the iron down, lifted the uniform top and sniffed it, looking at me over the top of the pink fabric. "Yes. Her grandson is your age. Did you meet him at school?"

"Fred."

"Yes! He's such a nice boy, so polite. I don't know how he turned out so well coming from that family. I guess the grandfather was some kind of shady character before he won a big lottery jackpot ten years ago, but Old Lady Spencer acts like she's some kind of American royalty."

"I overheard something about his brother today," I said.

Mom pulled the uniform top over her t-shirt. "Yeah, Stephen. He's a professional golfer. Linda talks about him all the time. Frankly, I get kind of sick of pretending I give a flying fadoodle about golf, but it makes her happy. I just wish he'd visit her more; you know, do something besides hit little white balls to deserve her adulation."

Linda was Mom's paraplegic client. She'd injured her back in a car wreck that had killed her husband. Fred's father, I supposed.

Mom headed for the front door.

"Where are you going?"

Her brows dropped. "I'm going to knock on every door in the complex and ask very sweetly if anyone 'accidently' took my laundry."

"Mom! You can't do that. What if the thief is some scary guy? What if it's that big hairy man across from us?" Our nearest neighbor was a thrice-divorced unemployed mechanic that looked at my plump but pretty mom with predatory eyes. If he took her clothes, I shuddered to think what he planned to do with her delicates.

"Then I'll kick his ass."

Mom was bluffing, of course. She wasn't in any way tough enough to do more than give someone a thorough talking to.

I sighed and shrugged back into my coat. "I'll go with you."

We'd talked to about five people after knocking on about twenty doors when we came to Mrs. Zimmerman's house. She was a retired guard from a women's prison and played in Gramma Foster's Friday night bridge club.

"Hi Martha," Mom said. "Listen, we didn't stop by to chat, it's just that someone took my laundry and I wondered, since you've got a good view of the laundry room from here, if you saw anything."

"Didn't see a thing," Mrs. Z. said in the raspy voice that gave testament to a lifetime of smoking.

"Okay. Sorry to bother you." Mom turned away, but I stood my ground as Mrs. Z. took out a cigarette and lit it.

I was absolutely certain that Martha Zimmerman was lying.

Mom said, "Tainie, come on."

My heart started pounding. Mrs. Z. was a big woman. She wasn't young, but I had no doubt she could flatten me in any altercation. Still, I could see mom's laundry in her mind, see it in a pile on the old prison guard's unmade bed.

"Tainie?"

I wanted to leave. But I also wanted to silence the certainty in my mind—prove to myself that these flashes of insanity were just that—and not some kind of impossible sixth sense I'd suddenly developed.

"I need to use your restroom," I said, and before Mrs. Z. could react, I bolted inside.

"Hey!"

I'll give it to Mrs. Z., for a large woman, she moved fast. Her condo was the same floor-plan as Gramma Foster's, though, and I knew which room was the master bedroom. I threw the door open just before she reached me. She threw me up against the door frame.

"You little…" Mrs. Z. said furiously as my mom came up from behind, yelling, "Tainie! What are you doing?"

Mom got a good look at the pile of pink clothing on the bed. Mrs. Z. quickly pulled the door closed and grated, "Get out."

Mom didn't budge. "Was that my stuff?"

"No, it was not. Now you take your rude little brat and get out of my house."

Mrs. Z. was several inches taller and an entire penal-system career rougher than my mom. For a frightening moment, I thought Mom was going to push the issue anyway. Instead, she backed away. When we got to the threshold, Mom said, "I need those uniforms to make my living, Martha."

"Not. Yours," Mrs. Z. snarled. We jumped back to avoid the banging of the door.

Mom looked at me. I expected her to be angry, but she asked, "How did you know?"

I shrugged the shoulder nearest to her as we began walking along the sidewalk, but she wouldn't drop it. "Honey, are you okay?"

"Depends on what you mean by okay," I mumbled.

She blocked my way with her body so I had to stop. I stared down at the scummy green puddle of water at the bottom of the pool.

"Tell me," Mom said.

I looked up into her concerned eyes and felt my own well up with tears. "I think I'm going crazy."

"Why?"

"I keep…thinking I can read people's minds."

Mom drew in a sharp breath. Her face had frozen into what looked like a horrified mask. Through lips that hardly moved, she asked, "How often has this happened?"

The tears spilled over and I dropped my chin to my chest. "Not all the time."

"What else?"

Surprised that she knew there was more, I said, "There was this other weird—incredibly weird—thing."

"Tainie, would you just tell me, please."

I felt a tickle as my nose began to run, and sniffed. "Okay. The other night my face changed. I was brushing my teeth and all of a sudden I had, like, a perfect mouth."

Mom staggered back and placed a hand on the wall to steady herself. "Oh, my God."

"What?" I exclaimed. "What does it mean?"

She didn't answer, just quickly scanned the courtyard as if making sure we hadn't been overheard and then grabbed my arm and practically dragged me up the stairs. In the condo, she glanced over at Gramma Foster, who was involved in one of her soap operas, and pulled me into the bedroom.

In a frantic whisper, she asked, "Did you touch the crown?"

I opened my mouth to say, "What?" but then I realized what she meant.

It was during that boat trip on the North Sea. I'd been so sick and had no sleep whatsoever. After dawn, when everyone gathered on deck, I was barely conscious of the reverent mood. I'd finally figured out that they were all there, as were Mom and I, to perform some kind of ludicrous ceremony that was supposed to stop the Cataclysm. We all gathered around a petite red-headed woman as the deck swayed and I tried not to dry heave.

The woman put a silvery circlet crown on her head and said, "Let us speak with the Gossamer Sphere." Everyone but me closed their eyes. No chanting, nothing but some hand-holding and everyone with this look on their face like they were in ecstasy or constipated or something. Under the all-pervading sense of nausea, I was embarrassed. Mortified really, that my mom was participating in this charade. It was inconceivable that she'd hauled me halfway around the world with her for this nonsense.

Everyone stood there with their eyes closed, concentrating on who knew what when the sky began to go purple. But that'd been happening a lot lately. I was the only one who saw it when the red-headed woman keeled over in an undignified sprawl on the deck. I ducked under some guy's arm and tried to help her. She was lying face-down, so I turned her head to make sure she was breathing.

Now Mom was asking me if I'd touched 'the crown,' and she could only mean the crown the redhead had been wearing. My palm had come into contact with it and I'd felt a weird sensation, like sticking my tongue on a battery, only ten times worse. I backed off, and just then everyone started to come out of whatever phony trance they'd been in. The sky looked like one of those big swirly rainbow lollipops at the circus.

Mom was standing by the bedroom door, tense and nervous-looking. "Did you, Tainie? Please tell me you didn't touch it."

In the smallest of voices, I asked, "Was I not supposed to?"

Chapter Seven

Mom hesitated for a second, and then lunged at me. I instinctively recoiled, but all she did was wrap her arms around me in an almost violent hug.

"You're alive," she whispered near my ear. "You survived initiation."

I struggled out of her grasp, exasperated. It was becoming clear to me that this was more of Mom's Fae garbage. "What are you talking about?"

She sighed. "It's complicated and I have to get to work. Walk with me."

Before I could respond, she left the bedroom. I followed slowly, loathe to hear what she had to say. Okay, yeah, I'd been experiencing some weird stuff lately, but not Mom weird. She took weird to a whole 'nother level.

The rain had stopped, but the sky hung heavy with ominous-looking clouds. The wind had picked up, too. Neither of us had an umbrella, and I hoped Mom didn't expect me to accompany her the entire way. The big house, practically a mansion, was over a mile away, and part of that was through a copse of woods that I didn't particularly care for. I'd walked this way with Mom once before, because as she'd put it, "In case there's an emergency and the phones are down, you need to know where I'll be."

It was two blocks before she took a deep breath and launched into her explanation.

"Your father was one of the folk."

I took this to mean Mom thought he was a fairy or an elf or some other magical being. The conversation had not begun well. Mom continued.

"There's a lot of superstition attached to it all, but I had the honor of speaking to Caitlin, the Last Noble, after we stopped the Gossamer Sphere. She's had two thousand years to study the situation and says that there's a scientific explanation to why the folk can shapeshift."

She was talking gobbledy-gook now, and my mind began to wander. We were passing a park with a wooden playground structure. A gust of wind bent a nearby sapling almost horizontal. About a hundred yards ahead, three teen boys were playing basketball on a fenced-in court.

"Are you listening to me?"

"Yeah, sure," I said. "I'm the daughter of a fairy. Go on."

She treated me to a pugnacious glare as we walked. "I knew you wouldn't listen. You never have. But this is important, Tainie!"

We were close enough to the basketball court now that the boys could hear her. One of them stopped playing and turned.

"Hey, Mrs. Strauss," he called.

Mom smiled. "Oh, hi Fred."

I wanted to sink into the sidewalk as Fred trotted to the chain-link fence. Despite the cold, his grey t-shirt had dark sweat stains under the arms. "Hi, Tainie."

I lifted my hand in a diffident wave and tried to walk faster.

"How's your mom today?" Mom asked. Thankfully, she didn't stop walking to chat.

"She's alright, but Gramma's on the rampage. Whatever you do, don't mention the smell. General Lee took a dump in the middle of the Chinese carpet in the entryway."

I knew that General Lee was the dog; a pure-bred St. Bernard that Mom said was nearly unmanageable.

She laughed. "I won't. Thanks for the heads-up."

Once we left the basketball court behind, she said, "He is *such* a nice boy," as if she hadn't just informed me I was the spawn of some kind of magical creature. I hoped that meant she wasn't going to pursue the subject any further, but I was disappointed.

Mom stepped off the sidewalk onto the thin dirt path that led into the wooded area. The shortcut took about a quarter mile off the walk, but it was spooky among the tall evergreen trees, especially with the howling wind.

"Alright," Mom said. "This is what I'm going to do. I'm going to try and get hold of Seamus—he's—well, technically, he's your uncle. After the Cataclysm, all the folk went back into hiding, of course, so it might take some time to find him, but if I borrow Mrs. Wharton's computer, I can send him an email at his old address. Maybe he's still checking it."

Through the branches of the trees, lightning flashed, followed less than five seconds later by a boom of thunder. I shoved my hands into the pockets of Gramma Foster's coat and hunched my shoulders. The path, layered with a thick carpet of fallen pine needles, petered out at the bank of a picturesque stream. We crossed over on some strategically placed boulders. On the other side, the trees thinned out quickly to reveal a sweeping expanse of lawn that was mostly green even though spring hadn't yet sprung.

I trudged behind Mom as she skirted the grass, following the line of trees toward the side of the big yellow house that looked like it had been built a century or so ago. Another close lightning strike heralded the rain. A cold, fat drop hit the part in my hair.

"Until we find someone who can tell us what to expect," Mom said, walking faster now, "promise me you won't try to experiment with your powers."

I wouldn't have suppressed the derisive laugh that burst out of me even if I could. I wanted to shout, I wanted to scream at her, "Stop it! Stop with the insane fairy tales!" But part of me almost wanted it to be true—the part that had no explanation for the strange, impossible things that had happened to me. Instead, I said, "Mom, I gotta head back now. It's raining, okay?"

We stopped in the cobbled courtyard that led to the side door 'servant's entrance.' She put an icy hand on my cheek and rested it there for a moment. A blast of frigid air swirled a handful of fallen leaves around us. The rain began to fall in earnest.

"I'm so sorry, sweetie. I should have prepared you better for this, but you haven't exactly been open to it, and besides, the odds of you actually becoming a shapeshifter were so slim…"

She leaned in like she was going to hug me, but I'd had enough. I spun around and shot off across the grass towards the trees. I heard her call something after me, but the wind blew her words away.

I had powers now? That's what she wanted me to believe? She'd said I was a shapeshifter. What was that supposed to even mean?

I thought about how my face had appeared to partially morph into Jessica's mouth and chin. Mom had just confirmed that it wasn't a hallucination. I didn't imagine it.

Impossible.

Hot tears trailed down my cold cheeks, mixing with the rain that soon soaked me through. A glance over my shoulder told me Mom was still watching, so I kept walking until I entered the forest, only stopping when I reached the stream. I sat cross-legged on a rock near the bank and watched the water tumble over the stony creek bed. Under the protection of the trees, only the occasional raindrop found me.

I held my hand out in front of my face. Shift, I thought. Change shape.

Nothing at all happened to my stubby fingers. I examined the weak fingernails that always split before they grew even a quarter-inch long, thinking about Mrs. Firestone back home. She was the drama teacher at my old high school, a former ballerina with long, graceful limbs. She would wave her hands around when she lectured, like fluttering white flower petals. My hand began to tingle just like my face had when it morphed, and panic set in.

I scrambled to my feet atop the rock and jumped to the ground. The flat-topped boulders that were sunk into the streambed as a path across the water weren't submerged by the rising creek yet, but they were wet, the storm-swollen water foaming near their uneven surfaces. I was so freaked out and so intrinsically clumsy anyway, the path could have been dry and level and I still probably would have slipped. Halfway across, my right foot skidded on the slick rock and I lost my balance. Rather than do a belly-flop, I jumped. My lower half sank into the water up to my waist and I gasped at the bitter chill. I clawed at the boulder, but the swift current dislodged me. Before I realized the significance of my situation, I was submerged up to my chin. I managed to get one quick breath before Gramma Foster's thick wool coat dragged me under.

Chapter Eight

I did not know how to swim. Mom had taken me to the Y for lessons one year, but I stubbornly clung to the side and refused to let go. If I'd been old enough to understand my fear better, I might have been able to articulate how uncomfortable the water made me feel. I felt safest under the warm, close quarters of my bedcovers—the cool, open expanse of pool water terrified me.

"What if someday you fall into the water and there's no one around to save you?" Mom tried to reason with my young self.

"I won't fall into the water," I remembered saying with a shrug, as if my logic trumped her worry.

The creek water wasn't deep, but it was fast and it was cold, and my shoes refused to find a firm purchase on the slippery rocks. I fought against the current, but felt myself being swept downstream. And there was the little matter of being unable to get my head back above water. My lungs burned.

I thrashed about, banging my knees and hands against the rocks. Finally, I rolled over and somehow my butt bounced off the creek bed enough for my face to pop out of the water. I sucked in a breath and tried again to stand. This time, I got to my feet long enough to take one step towards the shore before crashing down. I let out a scream, abruptly cut off as water filled my mouth and nose.

I realized at that moment that I was in actual danger of drowning. The whole shapeshifter thing was suddenly in sharp perspective. If only I knew how, I would embrace the ability right then and there to save myself.

A fish. I needed to turn myself into a fish!

My eyes were open to the murky water, my hands scrabbling for a handhold as I again began to run out of air. I thought of a fish I'd once seen in the giant tank at my dentist's office. It was long and sleek and had silvery scales and I was pretty sure it was the fresh-water variety. I focused on the image in my mind and felt that odd tingle overcome my whole body, but nothing happened. I didn't know the rules. I was going to die because there were limits to this ability and I had no idea what they were.

I tried again, thinking of an otter this time. Brown fur, lean body, whiskers! The water, which had been a greenish blur, became clear. I knew it had worked, knew I was now an otter, but I couldn't get to the surface because I was trapped in my human clothes. Otters had a large lung capacity, but they were air breathers and I'd been deprived too long. My webbed claws tore at the thick wet wool of my coat and I beat at the water with my strong tail, attempting to swim free.

Then I felt something else. Something had a hold of me, was lifting me! I tried to get away, my body squirming and undulating like never before. My pants slipped off, my head rose above the water, and I was eye-to-eye with Fred, who let out a shout and dropped me unceremoniously back into the creek.

Oh, shoot—*oh shoot*! I can't be an otter—he can't see me as an otter!

My otter body came fully free of the last of my clothing as I concentrated on changing back, but the face and body I imagined now wasn't the awkward, ugly one I'd been trapped in since the day I was born.

I tried to stand, but my shoes were gone and the rocks cut cruelly into my bare soles. I was floating further downstream and the water seemed deeper. My flailing struggles weakened even as I grew frantic again for air. Was Fred still there? Or had the encounter with the huge otter dressed in human clothing freaked him out enough that he'd given up looking for me? I extended my hand until it broke the surface of the water and I held it there as best I could.

The water was so cold. I saw the faint glow of the sky through the rippling surface, so close. There must be a break in the trees up there. The edge of my vision was going black.

Fred hadn't given up, thank goodness. My hand was grasped and yanked and my head came out of the water for the final time. He was strong; strong enough to battle the current and the cold and guide me to shore as I filled my lungs with oxygen. I wasn't too exhausted to feel the sting of mortification at being full-on naked, but there was nothing I could do about it but cross my arms over my chest.

Well, it wasn't *my* chest; that was patently clear as soon as my forearms came into contact with my much-smaller breasts. They were easier to cover than my own, as I stumbled on injured feet onto the bank and sank into a body-hiding crouch, coughing. His t-shirt was cold and wet, but when Fred draped it across my back, I gave him a grateful look.

"Are you okay?" he asked.

I nodded, not trusting my voice, which I was pretty sure would sound to Fred suspiciously like Tainie Strauss' voice, even though my face was radically different. If the shift was successful, and I was certain somehow that it had been, I was now the spitting image of an anonymous model I'd once seen in a magazine. Her huge blue eyes, small, pert nose and pouty lips had burned themselves into my mind as the epitome of beauty.

There was nothing else for me to do, I reached up and weakly pulled the sopping fabric from my back and tried to put his t-shirt on, but my fingers were too stiff from the cold. He knelt down in front of me and parted the fabric. Between us, we managed to pull the garment over my head. I thrust my arms through and pulled it down over my body. It came to mid-thigh, covering my nakedness.

He was still there in front of me, running his eyes over me with concern and something else. Something I'd never seen directed at me before, and never expected to see in my lifetime.

Interest.

Lust, even, if I was honest with myself. Fred Spencer, handsome rich kid, nice kid, as my mom would say, was looking at me that way. I was shivering from the cold, but felt a burn begin in my cheeks.

"Come on," he said, standing and holding out his hand. "My house is real close."

I stood up and immediately let out a cry of pain. Through the cold-induced numbness, the cuts and bruises I'd sustained on the bottom of my feet were making themselves known.

I knew he was going to do it before shirtless, wet, gorgeous Fred bent and scooped me up into his arms. That was the moment I fell in love with him.

Chapter Nine

He carried me all the way to his house, through the wind and the rain, without so much as a grunt of effort or protest. My hands clung to his neck and I had a hard time keeping my fingers from caressing the short hairs there. My cheek rested against his chest and if I turned only slightly, I could press my lips to his skin, which smelled spicy and musky despite his dousing in the creek. I resisted the urge, but it was difficult.

As soon as we got inside, he yelled, "Mrs. Strauss!" and my romantic notions instantly deserted me. Fred set me on a divan in the entryway. My mom thumped down the stairs, took one look at us and said, "I'll get some towels."

She hurried down a hallway. From a wide, arched doorway, an elderly lady appeared. This must be Fred's grandmother, Old Lady Spencer. She had the typical old lady coif, short white hair with a faint tinge of blue, permed, curled and teased to within an inch of its life. Her suit was Chanel, or so I thought, having recognized the style from a popular cartoon. Her black-rimmed eyes, with that tight skin around them that screamed 'facelift!' widened at the sight of us. Me, sitting with Fred's t-shirt stretched down over my knees and he standing there looking shell-shocked. The old lady's eyes focused disapprovingly on a spot under me and I glanced down. A puddle had formed on the polished wood floor. When Mom reappeared with an armload of towels, I expected the old lady to snatch them away and apply them to the growing puddle.

"My goodness, what happened?" Mom said. She handed a towel to Fred and draped one around my shoulders, looking into my face with not the faintest scrap of recognition. There was a mirror on the wall behind where the Old Lady was standing, but even if my sore feet would allow me to do so, getting up to check my appearance would seem to be the height of vanity. Fred was still standing there staring at me bemusedly, and I wasn't about to do anything to risk wiping that look off his face.

"I heard a scream," he said, glancing at Mom before looking back at me. "I saw a body in the water, but when I jumped in to help, there was this—this giant otter wearing clothes…"

"An otter? In our creek?" The old lady's amazement at the phenomenon didn't seem to extend to the fact that the otter was fully clothed.

"Yeah." Fred sounded less sure as I returned his gaze with a look that said I'd been too busy drowning to notice any larger-than-normal aquatic animals in the vicinity, dressed or otherwise.

Mom placed a hand on his forehead. "You're chilled to the bone. I want you upstairs and in a hot shower right away, Mister." She turned to the Old Lady as if she realized the order was overstepping her authority.

"Yes, Frederick, please go clean up. I'll see to it that Miss-"

She directed an inquiring look my way and I stuttered "Ta–Tai…" not your real name, stupid! "Tory."

"I'll make sure Tory gets a ride home."

"No!" Fred's blue eyes were intense. "I mean, I want to know how you got in the stream, and how that otter got into your coat, and—and–" His eyes shifted to my bare legs, which were long and shapely, the feet slender. I heard his unspoken, *Why were you naked*?

The Old Lady put a hand on his shoulder. "Now, Frederick…" she began.

Mom dared to interrupt her, "Wait a minute. How big was this otter?" I didn't have to see her face to know that she'd suddenly gotten very suspicious. If I didn't do something fast to change the direction of the conversation, she would certainly figure out who I was and what I'd done. I was quite possibly the worst liar on the planet, however, and if General Lee hadn't trotted into the entryway right then, I'm sure I would've given myself away.

The St. Bernard saw Fred and let out a low *wuff*. Barreling forward, claws clattering on the floor, he snuffled Fred's midsection briefly and then, without warning, hurled himself upon me.

"General Lee!" The Old Lady's cultured accent give way to a southern screech. "You naughty, naughty dog! Put him out, Fred."

I cringed beneath the hairy, slobbery behemoth as Fred grappled with his collar.

Over the commotion, a booming male voice sounded. "What's all this?"

Fred finally got the upper hand and dragged General Lee a few feet away. A dark-haired man with distinguished-looking silver sideburns frowned down on the scene. His blue eyes, very like Fred's, but much harder, cut to my legs. When the dog had jumped on me, his paws had pushed the hem of the shirt up to an indecent level. I hastily pulled it back down again, blushing furiously.

"That damned dog of yours, Walter!"

"Forget the dog, why are these two children half-naked and soaking wet in my hallway?" Walter Spencer was standing five feet away, but I could smell the liquor on his breath.

Fred's face contorted, I wasn't sure if it was in anger or chagrin, but he, too, raised his voice. "Because she almost drowned!"

"Then why hasn't anyone called an ambulance? She looks fine, that's why." The elder Mr. Spencer's voice dropped and took on a gravelly snideness. "The little tart laid in wait for you, boy, can't you see that? She took off her clothes and jumped in the creek so you'd save her. These girls can't snag Stephen, so they go for the next best thing."

I felt my mouth drop open and stay that way.

"Do you really think so?" The Old Lady asked, sounding incredulous, but her sneer told me the idea had already taken root. "Maybe instead of an ambulance, we should call the police."

Fred was still trying to control General Lee, who hadn't been subdued just because he'd been thwarted from mauling me.

Mom had been standing back, watching from a safe distance. From the way she talked about this job, I knew she avoided calling attention to herself, but she took pity on me. "Nonsense. Drowning victims often shed their clothing to keep from being weighed down. Come with me, Tory. We'll get you to the bathroom and I'll find something dry for you to wear."

I stood up without thinking and winced at the pain in my feet. Mom put her arm around me and let me lean on her for the short walk to a guest bathroom on the main floor as Fred hauled the still struggling dog out of the entryway.

Mom left me in the bathroom and I finally got a good look at myself. Even soaked like a drowned rat, I was beautiful. I gazed at my reflection, hope and exultation rising in my breast.

Then I heard snatches of conversation, so I cracked the door and actively listened. At one end of the hall, I heard my mother, apparently on the telephone, asking, "She's not home yet?" At the other end of the hall, the elderly Spencer couple was still deciding whether to call the cops. "Well, sure dumping her pants and coat makes sense, but I could tell she wasn't even wearing…" the Old Lady's voice dropped to a dramatic whisper, "a bra!"

"Exactly my point," said Mr. Spencer. "How much could her underwear have weighed her down?"

I looked around the room. No window to escape out of. My mom now knew I hadn't made it home. The police may very well soon be on their way. I looked in the mirror again and had an epiphany.

Hairy. Slobbery. General Lee.

I watched it happen this time and had to dampen down the thrill of fascinated fear that came along with the change. I dropped my front paws to the floor and discovered that shapeshifting did nothing to alleviate the pain in my feet. I started for the door, which I'd wisely left cracked, but then I noticed I still had Fred's t-shirt on.

Shoot.

I wiggled my body along the floor, rubbed up against the cupboard under the sink, but the darned thing was not coming off without the aid of some fingers and an opposable thumb. I didn't know the rules for shapeshifting, assuming there were any, but hopefully it wouldn't hurt to do it back-to-back.

I changed back into myself, or rather, the new beautiful 'me,' in case anyone burst in on me. I pulled the shirt off, stashed it in the cupboard and opened the door a crack. Within moments I was back on the floor in my General Lee guise.

After nosing the door open, I looked up and down the hall, irritated that in order to see through the hair hanging in my eyes, I had to tilt my head this way and that. Plus, the world around me had taken on strange blue and yellow hues—I wasn't color blind exactly, but my doggie vision was not the same as my human. Mom's back was to me, Old Lady Spencer was wiping up the puddle Fred and I had made, and Fred's grandfather was nowhere to be seen. I trotted out nonchalantly.

The Old Lady must have acutely attuned ears because even though I did my best to walk without clicking my claws on the floor, she heard me anyway.

"Oh!" she exclaimed. "How did you–? Fred!"

That was my cue to exit stage left. I went the way I'd seen Fred take the dog, because it was clear I wasn't getting out the front door, but maybe Fred would see me, figure I'd gotten back in somehow, and let 'General Lee' out again. I rounded a corner and there Fred was, standing in front of some wide French doors. On the other side of the glass, General Lee barked and whined.

"Oh, this is not good," I said.

It came out of my canine snout sounding like a threatening growl.

To my absolute horror, Fred reached for a nearby candlestick and hefted it, eyes pinning me to where I stood.

Chapter Ten

I had to change the dynamic of the situation—fast. I had a tail now, and discovered I knew how to use it. Back and forth, back and forth as rapidly as I could, I wagged that tail. I opened my mouth and trailed my tongue out of the side in what I hoped was a good approximation of a doggy grin. Then I did what I'd seen other dogs do when they wanted to play: I spread my paws in kind of a bow and tried out a playful little bark.

It worked. Fred set the candlestick down, a perplexed look on his face. I trotted to the door and waited expectantly.

"You want out—strange doggie?" Fred asked. With a shrug, he opened the door.

I was now face-to-face with General Lee, but it wasn't my *face* the dog was interested in. He came in as I slipped out, giving him the perfect opportunity to thrust his cold, wet nose under my tail. A surprised yelp burst out of me and I tucked tail and ran.

I didn't get far. Of course putting General Lee out meant that the yard would have to be enclosed, or he'd be all over the neighborhood. I ran the length of the fence, looking for a place to escape. General Lee came right back out of the house and kept pace with me, barking. I got the impression he was still looking for a proper introduction—I'd been rude and hadn't allowed him to get a good whiff of my backend. A backend that, despite the fur and tail, felt exposed beyond belief.

The yard was big, the landscaping a mix of grass, groomed evergreen bushes and patches of garden that hadn't yet bloomed. Someone hadn't been scooping up after General Lee. My run around the wooden fence included some hopping and leaping over big mounds of excrement that assaulted my newly enhanced sense of smell.

It quickly became clear I was going to have to come up with another plan. As a dog, I'd never get out of this yard.

The rain began to seep into my undercoat. I ran along the side of the house, General Lee by my side, nipping at me now as he tried to get my attention. Here, there weren't any windows, which meant this was the garage side of the house.

It was now or never.

I stopped by the side gate and tried to focus, which was difficult since General Lee had apparently decided the chase around the yard was enough courtship for him; time to get to the good stuff.

"Gross! Get off me!" I yelled. It came out as a series of growling barks. For good measure, I snarled and snapped in General Lee's direction. He backed off, but didn't look deterred. I was a female St. Bernard in his territory—fair game!

I was glad the change only took a few seconds. I stood and reached for the gate latch, waiting for General Lee to get over the shock and confusion of my unexpected non-canine status and take a bite out of my now tail-less behind.

He didn't. I made it out, shut the gate and looked around. Best case scenario, I'd see a batch of fresh laundry hanging nearby on the line, but no. My choice of apparel seemed limited to handfuls of dried grass or a thorny bush or two. If I made a run for the woods, I'd have to cross in front of the house, and frankly, I had never been the type of person who could imagine herself streaking under any circumstances.

The only possible course was to become another animal, preferably something that wouldn't get chased or shot at. Unfortunately, I couldn't think of anything that would also plausibly be found wandering this particular neighborhood.

I changed back into General Lee. As soon as I did, I heard him begin barking madly on the other side of the fence.

I estimate it took me about fifteen minutes to make it to Gramma Foster's condo. The weather kept everyone indoors, and I met no one and nothing on the way. I started to climb the cement stairs, but my plan faltered. How on earth was I going to get in? Gramma kept the door locked at all times, and there was no key hidden under the mat. The disgusting man across the way kept his blinds open so he could look out. There's no way he wouldn't notice a naked girl banging on the door.

I turned and scanned the area. If I gathered up all the mats in front of our neighbor's doors, I might be able to fashion a truly hideous outfit of sorts. Mr. Perkins had an American flag flying, but it was only about a yard of fabric if I could even figure out how to tear it down. Then I saw the laundry room door on the other side of the pool.

When I got there, I heard the dryer running inside, so there was a chance whichever tenant was doing laundry had left the door unlocked. I couldn't very well open it with my paws, though. Just as I finished the change into the new, beautiful but buck-naked 'me,' Mrs. Zimmerman's door opened and she stepped out to light a cigarette. In one hand she held a bottle of cheap beer. She began scoping out her next-door neighbor's flower box for some reason, but I knew it was only a matter of time before she noticed me. She took a long swig of her beer, staggering back a bit like she was intoxicated, then she wiped her mouth with the back of her hand and dumped the rest of the beer into her neighbor's flowers.

I did the only thing I could think of, and when Mrs. Z. did glance over at me, she saw…herself. She saw herself, a smaller version and naked as a sow, open the laundry room door and disappear inside. I heard an angry bellow as I locked the door from the inside and rushed over to open the dryer. As the banging on the door began, I dressed in the first things that came to hand, a pair of too-big stretch pants and a sweatshirt with the words, "I survived the Cataclysm and all I got was this lousy t-shirt" on it. I recognized the shirt as belonging to a young woman in her twenties named Penny, the daughter of Mrs. Wharton in the condo below Gramma Foster.

When I opened the laundry room door, I was not me, not the new me, and not Mrs. Z. Penny gave Mrs. Z. a strange look and said, "Excuse me." Mrs. Z. barged into the small room and demanded, "Where is she?"

"Who?" I asked.

Mrs. Z. stared at Penny-me with furious eyes. "What kind of crap are you trying to pull?"

I gave her my best 'are you crazy?' look and shrugged.

Mrs. Z. was not the kind of person to let something like that go, but she must have been sufficiently drunk and befuddled, because she didn't accost me further. I made it to Gramma Foster's front door, and, with my face to the door so the nosy man across the way wouldn't witness it, changed into the real me.

Gramma opened the door and exclaimed, "There you are! Call your mother right this instant, young lady. She's worried sick."

I knew I could count on absent-minded, short-sighted Gramma Foster not to detect anything different about me, like the lack of shoes or coat, or the fact that my hair hung in stringy wet strands in my face.

I called Mom and gave her the story I'd made up on the way through the little forest—I'd run into a friend from school and we'd hung out at her house until the worst of the rain passed. She didn't sound convinced.

"Did you see anyone by the creek when you crossed? There was an—incident—with a girl who almost drowned."

"No. Like I said, I ran into Gina from school."

Mom's sigh carried clearly over the line. I was frankly amazed that she hadn't accused me of being the girl Fred brought home, especially since that girl had disappeared at the same time a General Lee look-alike had appeared in the Spencer household out of nowhere. Mom only said, "Alright. When I get home tomorrow morning we need to sit down and discuss…your situation, though, okay? I'm sure you have a lot of questions."

I felt the best way to hide my involvement in the 'incident' was to continue with my official stance on the shapeshifting topic. "Mom, I don't believe in that junk and I don't appreciate your trying to push it on me."

"Well, tough. We're talking about it and that's final."

I pretended to capitulate. "Fine. Just don't expect me to become a convert any time soon."

After hanging up, I excused myself to Gramma Foster and went into the bathroom to take a hot shower, using way too much of our rationed water.

All of my cuts and bruises made themselves known as I soaped myself down. When I got out, I wiped the steam from a patch of mirror. So many thoughts and emotions struggled for dominance behind my eyes. More than anything, I wished I could cast aside my real face and body from this day forward and live the life I'd always dreamed of living. There had to be a way to rid myself of Titania Strauss.

Chapter Eleven

Sleep eluded me for hours as I stared into the dark all agog with the day's revelations, my wild adventure, and especially the memories of being held in Fred's arms. That part kept playing over and over in my mind, like a steamy movie loop. It shouldn't have, I know it, but it even eclipsed the fact that I now had the ability to literally be anyone I wanted to be.

Well, sort of.

When I got up in the morning, even though I'd also lain awake trying to formulate a plan to use that ability, I didn't have one.

I couldn't show up at school looking gorgeous, nor could I even tidy up the worst of my facial deformities. Too many people had seen me up close to get away with that.

I couldn't invent another person and play both roles. That scenario might be perfectly plausible for the average movie-of-the-week, but the reality was: I had no way to create and register a whole 'nother person at my school, even if I could pull off being two people at once. The homework alone would kill me.

Mom was waiting for me at the little two-person table in the kitchenette. She didn't notice my backpack was bulkier than usual. I'd put Penny's t-shirt and stretch pants in a plastic grocery bag and tucked it in there, plus I borrowed Mom's only extra pair of shoes and her old windbreaker and stuffed them in, too, so she wouldn't ask about my own missing shoes—and Gramma's coat—which I had no idea how I was going to replace.

"Are you okay?" she asked.

I'd done my best to walk out normally in my stockinged feet, but they were killing me and my knees and legs were black and blue. If she caught sight of them in the next few weeks before the bruises faded, I'd be hard-pressed to come up with an explanation.

I forced a smile. "I'm fine."

Of one thing I was almost certain: if Mom knew I had already pretty much embraced the fact that I was a shapeshifter, she'd make me promise not to use the ability. I didn't have to read her mind to know it. She'd been prepping me my whole life to accept that I was born 'different.' And by that, I always assumed she meant 'ugly.' She'd been hell-bent on developing my more virtuous qualities, like honesty and intelligence, and preached constantly about the benefits of accepting my limitations.

The less she knew the better.

She smiled back at me, but it didn't reach her eyes. "Have a seat, sweetie. I made French toast. There's no maple syrup, but I found an old crystallized bottle of honey in the back of the cupboard. It just needed heating up and it's as good as new."

Natural sweeteners, including cane sugar, corn syrup, maple syrup and honey, were hard to come by these days. Blame it on the Cataclysm. Sugarcane crops in Brazil and elsewhere had been decimated, and the honeybee population, which had already been on a mysterious decline, had virtually disappeared. That made all the other sweeteners go up in price and down in availability.

I thanked her and sat, tucking into my meal like it was any other morning.

"I wanted to explain about your father," she said.

My head came up and I stopped chewing. I'd expected her to confront me about yesterday's incident, but it appeared she hadn't made the connection between me and the mystery girl. Yet.

"The night I met your father, I was at a nightclub in Seattle with some girlfriends. He approached me initially in his true form and asked me to dance, but I shot him down. I remember because the song 'Smells Like Teen Spirit' by Nirvana was playing and I told him I loved Kurt Cobain and just wanted to listen to it. So he left and then about ten minutes later this guy comes up to me and it's Kurt Cobain."

"That's a coincidence. Wasn't he married to, like, Courtney Love or something?"

"Yes, eat your French toast before it gets cold. So, there I was and there he was and, wow, you know, my friends couldn't believe Kurt Cobain was not only there, but he was totally into me."

"Yeah, but he was married."

"Would you forget that for a minute? I realize now that sleeping with a married man wasn't a good idea, except how can I regret that decision? If I hadn't have been young and stupid with stars in my eyes, I wouldn't have you."

I got up and poured myself a glass of apple juice. When I sat back down, Mom said, "A few days after it happened, the news reported that Kurt had killed himself, and when I found out that he couldn't possibly have been with me that night because he was already gone, I thought I'd been fooled by a look-alike. Just someone who resembled him and preyed on naïve fans who'd had too much to drink."

I ate my French toast and drank my juice, but Mom somehow inferred criticism anyway.

"Look, I'm not trying to justify what I did. It was completely and totally irresponsible of me. Not only did I go off with a total stranger, but I had unprotected s–"

"I got it, Mom!"

She shot me a reproachful look, but thankfully didn't expound any further on the details.

"To make a long story short," she continued, and I thought, too late, "I was going to nursing school at the time and found out I was pregnant and then your father shows up one day, only I didn't know he was your father, of course, and we became friends. It was a rough time for me and he helped me through a lot.

"When you were born, you were very sick. Fae babies mostly don't survive. But you did and your father had to tell me the truth. Then, God, I remember this like it was yesterday, he showed me."

Mom had tears in her eyes now. I poked my fork into the final bite and dragged it across my plate to sop up the last of the honey. She was struggling to pull herself together while I chewed it, and I was trying not to get sucked into her emotional state, so I spoke with my mouth full, "What'd you do?"

She uttered a bitter little laugh. "I freaked."

Just then I heard a sound from behind me and Mom looked up past my shoulder. "Good morning Edna. Did you sleep well?"

Gramma shuffled into view in her bathrobe and slippers, her thin white hair mussed. She held her arms out like a zombie and moaned, staggering to the coffee pot.

"Just one cup," Mom said and ignored the childish scrunch-face Gramma directed her way.

Mom turned back to me and sighed. Quietly, she said, "There's more, but we'll talk again after school, okay?"

I decided I actually wanted to hear the rest, so I said, "Okay."

Once Mom went to bed, I forced my aching size ten feet into her size eight shoes and zipped up the too-large wind-breaker. I'd minced my way down only a few of the cement stairs outside when I realized I wouldn't make it to school.

It occurred to me, as I stood there thinking about how a person could obtain a huge pair of shoes at seven in the morning with no money, that the problem for someone else might be the shoes, but not for me. I concentrated on Mom's feet. Her second toe didn't extend half an inch past her big one like mine did. The balls of her feet were narrow, unlike mine, which were wide enough to double as snowshoes. As I pictured her feet, I was careful not to focus on the rest of her. I just needed to borrow her little piggies. Within moments, the pain below my ankles eased.

I started back down again, but hesitated when I heard the banging of a slammed door and a female voice shout, "Fine!"

Penny, from the condo below us, whose clothes were burning a hole in my backpack, stomped by. Her blonde-streaked brown hair was pulled back in a ponytail and her pretty face was drawn and angry. I pressed my back into the railing, but she seemed distracted and probably wouldn't have noticed me anyway. As soon as she disappeared around the corner, I slunk over to the laundry room and slipped inside. I left Penny's clothes on the dryer with a note, "Whoops! These got into my load somehow." No signature, naturally.

I ended up a few minutes late to my first class.

"Next time, you'll need a tardy slip from the office," Mr. Collins said. I nodded and hurried down the aisle to my chair. Gina lifted her eyebrows at me and I soon saw why.

A dark, bulky lump covered my seat, part of it hanging down off the side, slowly dripping muddy water onto the floor. It took me a second to recognize Gramma Foster's coat. I raised my eyes to Fred, who was watching me intently. My heart began to pound.

Jessica giggled and whispered, "Gross." I could tell she was enjoying the spectacle as I picked up the wet and filthy coat with my fingertips and draped it on the back of the chair. She turned around to Fred and said, "Good one." He ignored her.

The coat wasn't all that unique, so I wondered how he knew it was mine until he reached into his backpack and partially pulled out one of my tennis shoes. He cocked an eyebrow, my signature smiley-face shoelace pinched between his fingers.

I ducked my head, swiped a hand across my seat to squeegee the worst of the moisture away and sat, leaning forward to avoid the wet wool.

Did he know?

Chapter Twelve

There's no way he could know. He obviously had his suspicions, but he didn't *know*.

Mr. Collins began lecturing and I took out my notebook, but not to jot down what my teacher was saying about the hero's journey. Instead, I made a list, written in code in case someone got hold of my notebook, of what Fred had seen yesterday. He didn't strike me as the kind of guy to jump to paranormal conclusions just because some strange stuff had happened. Just like me when my face first morphed and I began to read people's minds, he probably thought he was going nuts or was sick or something.

That reminded me. If I wanted to know what he thought, I had the means.

I hadn't actually tried to read anyone's mind before, though, and I wasn't sure exactly how to go about it. In the past, I'd simply wondered what any given person was thinking and their thoughts had just sort of been there for me to hear in my head. I tried to pick up on Fred's thoughts, but was afraid to concentrate too hard on it in case I shapeshifted into him. There had to be something that distinguished the two aspects of being, as my mom would say, 'Fae.'

"Miss Strauss, did you hear me?"

I looked up at Mr. Collins, shocked. He'd asked me a question and I had no idea what it was. I opened my mouth to apologize, but instead, I reached out somehow, staring into his eyes until I retrieved what I needed to know.

"The Call to Adventure?" I said, wording it like a question even though I knew it was the right answer.

"Very good, you *were* listening," Mr. Collins said. He moved on to the next victim and I smiled in relief.

The key, apparently, was that I needed to be looking directly at the person to read their mind. I wasn't about to turn in my seat and stare at Fred.

Besides, I was pretty sure the mind-reading was limited to the thoughts a person was having at that moment, and there was no guarantee he'd be thinking what I wanted to know. In fact, if I did turn to look at him, I'd probably be treated to another insult.

At the end of class, I waylaid him to offer up the simple, and ironic, explanation I'd invented.

"Thanks for finding my coat," I said. "Someone stole my stuff out of the laundry room."

I was looking at him now, so it was easy to eavesdrop on whether my story convinced him.

It did.

He was relieved that ugly Tatiana Strauss didn't have anything to do with the beautiful girl he'd rescued.

"I only found one shoe," he said.

"Bummer. Where'd you find it? Maybe I can find the other one after school." I had every intention of trying.

"The creek." He was already looking distractedly past me like he was done with the conversation. I took one last opportunity to peek into his mind.

His thoughts were a heated jumble of images: the near-naked girl in his arms (me!), her cold flesh smooth against his chest, her wet thighs firm against his forearm as he held her close. His memory produced a jolt throughout his lower body—and a corresponding response in mine.

I felt a hot blush suffuse my cheeks, but he didn't notice. He nodded in my direction and brushed past. I gingerly gathered Gramma's wet, dirty coat and left before the next student to sit in my seat arrived.

Ashworth Academy had rows of lockers lining the halls—lockers that sat empty like mocking monuments to a safer time. Years ago, the principal had banned their use, like other schools across the nation that somehow figured a gun carried around in a student's backpack was safer than one stored in a locker. Seemed to me it like it'd be easier to access a gun in a backpack in the event said student decided to go on a shooting rampage, but what did I know? Right then, walking the hall with Gramma's wet coat, I just wished I had somewhere to put it.

"Need this?" Gina appeared next to me. She'd rushed out of class as usual, but here she stood holding a black garbage bag. She shook it open and helped me stuff the coat inside while I effusively thanked her.

"No prob. The janitor doesn't lock his storage closet. I'm kinda surprised Fred would do something like that, he seemed nice."

"Oh, he didn't do it. He found it. The coat, I mean. It was in the creek." I realized I was babbling when I caught the skeptical look on Gina's face. I mumbled, "I don't know how it got there."

"Like I said, he seemed nice. If you want to believe he didn't do it, you go right ahead. But I'm tellin' you, that Jessica skeeze was mightily impressed with it."

As soon as Gina said "Jessica," I opened my mouth to stop her from finishing what she was saying—because Jessica and one of her friends had come to stand right behind her—but Gina rambled on so quickly I couldn't interrupt in time.

"What'd you say, bitch?" Jessica punctuated the word 'bitch' with a shove to Gina's shoulder that made her stumble forward into me. The blood drained out of Gina's face, but I saw her jaw tighten before she turned. Jessica was several inches taller and quite a bit more confident than Gina, plus, the one friend was suddenly joined by two other girls. All looked eager for a fight.

"I said," Gina began, speaking through clenched teeth, but the bell rang, and a teacher approached us, saying, "Break it up! Get to class, girls."

It was Mr. Applebee, our Chemistry teacher, and not even Jessica was going to gainsay him. She shot Gina a look that promised retribution before stalking off with her posse close behind.

"You girls okay?" Mr. Applebee asked. "Because it looked to me like something was going on here."

"We're fine," Gina said quickly. She grabbed my arm and dragged me away.

"I have to go the other direction," I protested as soon as we were out of earshot of Mr. Applebee.

"She's going to kill me!" Gina hissed. "You have to help me."

"What can I do?"

"Girls!" Mr. Applebee was still standing there watching us.

Gina's eyes were wild. "I don't know. Help me think of something at lunch, okay?"

I nodded and she shot off down the hall, head down and arms crossed. I had to walk back past Mr. Applebee to get to class.

"We don't tolerate bullying here," he said softly, one bushy red eyebrow lifted. "But we can't help if you don't tell us what's going on."

I offered him a tepid smile as I slunk on by with my garbage bag full of wet coat. "Thanks. I'll keep that in mind."

In the cafeteria at lunch, I lurked by the entrance looking for Gina and fighting off a nagging feeling of resentment. Yes, Jessica had already picked on me and maybe there was no way either of us, me or Gina, could have avoided getting on her bad side. Ha, if she even had a good side. Still, I wondered if it was worth it to have a friend like Gina. I may be lonely, but she had a big mouth, and it had gotten her, and me by association, into a world of trouble three whole days into the school year.

It wasn't like I didn't already have my own share of trouble.

The smell of greasy pizza hung in the air and made my stomach growl. I saw Tamika sitting at one of the neutral tables—a step up from the Loser table of yesterday. She acted like she didn't see me and I didn't blame her. News travelled through school like wildfire; surely rumor of the impending skirmish had reached her. She didn't deserve to be sucked into this predicament. Yesterday she'd offered me solidarity, but yesterday I'd been a simple Loser. Today I was toxic.

Jessica was in line for hot food, surrounded by girls who, it seemed to me, were all there to support her. Afraid one of them would tag me as Gina's one and only sidekick, I left.

Gina was outside, sitting on the side of the empty fountain, looking forlorn. When she saw me, she rushed over and said, "Did you see her? Did she say anything to you?"

"Yeah, she's in the cafeteria. No, she didn't see me. Come on, let's go to my house for lunch." Gramma Foster would be surprised to see us, but I didn't think she'd mind.

We began walking, and I have to admit I was scared. I knew Jessica had a tray full of food that she would most likely sit and eat, surrounded by her friends and admirers, but I couldn't help feeling like she was going to run up behind us any second.

It would have been sunny out today if it weren't for the Cataclysm haze. I saw a patch of cheerful-looking dandelions, growing like they didn't know they were weeds, and one of the trees we passed had tiny buds on it. The prospect of spring brought my spirits up slightly.

Gina seemed as gloomy as ever. The one time I glanced over at her while we walked, it looked like she was about to burst into tears, so I kept silent.

There were kids walking in all directions away from the school. Not far ahead of us, I noticed two young men. The slight *ting ting* of a basketball bouncing on the sidewalk reached me on the light breeze. I knew it was Fred even before he stopped and waited for us to catch up. His friend, the same blonde kid I always saw him with, kept on walking and bouncing the ball.

A dark blue convertible Mustang pulled up to the curb, music blaring. Fred was still several yards away when he took my shoe out of his backpack and said, "I forgot to give you this."

He tossed it to me, but it fell short and bounced off a patch of dead grass before rolling into the gutter. He made a chagrined face, but didn't attempt to retrieve it for me. I realized why when the music stopped and the driver, a handsome young man who appeared to be in his early twenties, called out, "Get in, butthead!"

Fred didn't want the driver of the cool car to see him associating with me. I shrugged to myself and thought, *whatever*. He jumped into the backseat as I fished my shoe out of a pile of dead leaves. The tires screeched a bit as the driver popped the clutch before performing a sharp U-turn in the street. As they drove past, I was surprised to see Penny in the passenger seat. She was staring ahead of her blankly.

Chapter Thirteen

Over a lunch of Triscuits and cheese, Gina and I came up with a plan. Well, actually I thought of it. Gramma Foster had been bustling around the kitchen when we first got home, griping about all the vitamin supplements my mom made her take. It gave me an epiphany.

"We need to think about this in a different way," I said.

"How so?" Gina asked.

"Well, how about instead of waiting for Jessica to make the first move, we pre-empt her?"

Gina took a bite. "I'm listening."

"She's always drinking bottled water, right?" I asked.

"They all do." She rolled her eyes. I took 'they' to mean Jessica and her friends. "I heard her going on about how water is like a fat flush."

"Flush, heh," I said, thinking of how flushed Gramma had gotten the other day when she took too much niacin. "Well, do you think you can slip something into her drink in Chemistry class?"

Gina's exaggerated frown affected every aspect of her face. "I'm not going to drug her, are you crazy?"

"Shh!" I tilted my head toward the living room, where Gramma was placidly knitting and watching television, as always.

"So…what are you talking about here?" Gina asked. "Some of your grandmother's medicine? I'd rather let Jessica beat me up than get busted for something like that."

I got up and nonchalantly read the labels on several bottles sitting on the counter. I opened one and dumped a few white tablets into my palm. Back in my seat at the little table, I leaned conspiratorially forward and whispered, "Trust me."

Coming up with a harebrained scheme was the easy part. Enacting it was something different altogether.

We'd crushed the niacin into a fine powder using a spoon and transferred it to an envelope. In Chemistry class, I watched as Gina sat on her stool, ignoring the baleful looks Jessica cast her way. The girls were sitting right up front, but it seemed to me that Mr. Applebee hovered around them, probably in an effort to stave off the chick fight he suspected was about to break out any minute.

Jessica's ever-present bottle of water was within Gina's reach, but it might as well have been in deepest Africa for all the opportunity she had to grab it, open it, dump the powder in, close it and shake it up. All before Jessica or anyone else saw what she was up to.

This was going to be harder than I thought.

We were supposed to be working on an experiment. I was distracted, so I let Fred do all the work while I jotted down half-hearted notes. More than once I saw Gina slide her hand toward the water bottle, but pull it away at the last second.

"What's she trying to do?" Fred said in my ear, startling me so badly I nearly fell off my stool.

"Wh-who?"

"Your friend. You've been scoping her out since class started and she keeps reaching for Jessica's water. Is she trying to spike it with something?"

My guilt must have been all over my face because he laughed and said, "I'm in."

Before I could ask him what he meant, he slid off his stool and walked over to Mr. Applebee, who happened to be standing to the left of Jessica. I didn't hear what Fred said, but Jessica's attention had been successfully diverted. She stared at Fred like he was a double-dipped chocolate cone on a hot summer premenstrual day. I waved surreptitiously to Gina, who grabbed the water. From where I sat, I couldn't see what she did because it was blocked by her body, but in less than ten seconds, the water was innocently back on the counter.

I glanced around at the other students, none of whom seemed to have noticed.

Except Fred. I heard him thank Mr. Applebee, and as he walked back to our station, he winked at me.

Then Jessica, whose throat must have gone dry while ogling Fred, took a big long swig of water. I saw Gina turn away to hide her delight.

"So what's in the water?" Fred asked quietly.

"Niacin."

He shook his head at me, so I explained the side effects.

"Wow, that oughta freak her out enough to keep her from beating Gina up after school, but what about tomorrow?"

So he'd heard. Probably everyone in school knew. And he was

right—no matter how underhanded we were, we couldn't stave off the inevitable forever.

Chapter Fourteen

Watching Jessica go into hysterics when the niacin kicked in wasn't as satisfying as I thought it would be. She made such a fuss, Mr. Applebee sent her to the school nurse, who promptly called an ambulance. Then there was talk that she'd gotten contaminated by one or more chemicals in the Chemistry lab, so we were all evacuated.

"Cool," Fred said. "Too bad there's only five minutes left in class."

The hospital would probably draw her blood to test for whatever the usual suspects were in cases sudden of rash. I doubted they'd test for niacin, but I had no way of knowing. The one thing I did have control over was preventing anyone from testing Jessica's water bottle. In her rush to leave for the nurse's office, she'd left it sitting there.

I snagged it on the way out and dropped it in the nearest trash can. Gina found me in the hall soon after and said, "It worked!"

We giggled all the way outside and halfway home, plotting what to do next.

"Oh! Oh! I know where some poison ivy grows near the creek," she said, with an almost maniacal laugh.

"No way!" I exclaimed.

"We'll get her in English, rub it all over her desk!"

I laughed so hard I snorted. We'd gone from marked 'men' to successful saboteurs in one afternoon.

"Okay, my house is this way," Gina said, pointing down the cross street a block before Gramma's complex. "I'll go home and get some heavy-duty gloves. Meet me by the basketball court in half an hour and we'll harvest us some rash that won't wear off."

Buoyant from the unaccustomed laughter, I agreed. Once we'd parted ways, though, doubts began to surface. The niacin side-effect would have faded well before Jessica got to the doctor. We might have gotten away with today's shenanigans, but a poison ivy rash would last for days, and a doctor could easily diagnose it. Plus, every kid who sat at her desk in later periods would end up with a rash, too, so the source would be easy to identify. It wouldn't take Jessica long to figure out who was responsible.

Still, I'd promised. Once I got home, I changed into an outfit more suited to stealthy doings—a pair of black pants and a black long-sleeved sweater. Even though I told Gina I'd meet her in half an hour, I left sooner in order to avoid Mom when she woke up. I did want to find out more about my father and my heritage, but at the same time, I was leery. I had the nagging feeling Mom was going to tell me something I really didn't want to hear.

"Gramma, I'm going to a friend's house to study," I said.

She asked, "On the third day of school? What are they teaching you at that place?"

"Chemistry."

"Oh, all right…" she said vaguely.

I was kind of hoping to see Fred at the basketball court, but no one was there, not even Gina. I walked slowly up and down the sidewalk for half an hour before concluding that she wasn't coming. If I waited any longer, I'd be a sitting duck when Mom came by on her way to work.

I did need to find my other shoe, however, so I headed for the woods. There was plenty of light, but the trees still gave me the creeps. I worried that homeless people might like to camp out in places like this; solitary, yet nearby homes where they could steal things. With that in mind, I peered into dark places and tried to walk noiselessly. That was how I saw Fred before he saw me.

He was perched on one of the boulders on the other side of the creek, chucking stones into the water. I ducked behind the nearest tree and froze. Part of me wanted to scurry back the way I'd come, run home to the safety of my bed. The familiar, lonely safety. The rest of me knew this was my chance—my first opportunity to be someone other than the unattractive, socially awkward girl I'd always been—but wasn't, as it turned out, born to be.

I shifted into the face and body of the girl he'd rescued and braced myself to step out from behind the tree trunk. But when I glanced down at my clothes, I realized there was no way I could approach him without a major undergarment adjustment. Under the snug fabric of the black sweater, the wrinkled hills and valleys of my deflated bra mocked me. I wondered about that for a moment, wondered why when I'd changed into an otter, it had been a huge otter. I was now taller, yet slimmer than normal, but my basic body mass was the same. The shapeshifting was probably limited by size—if I tried to become a mouse, for instance, it would be an awfully big mouse.

I reached up under my shirt and unhooked the bra, then pulled my arms out of the sleeves and into the shirt to remove the straps. When I'd extricated myself from it, I held the utilitarian, formerly white brassiere I'd had since middle school, at a loss as to what to do with it. I finally wadded it up and thrust it into an evergreen bush.

I took a deep breath, stiffened my spine and stepped out onto the path.

Fred was gone.

There was no sign of him anywhere. The air left my lungs in a disappointed whoosh and I stood there looking out past the creek, past the line of trees bordering his parent's property. I could see a sliver of green grass, but other than the hypnotic waving of the trees in the wind, nothing moved.

I briefly considered walking up to his door and ringing the bell.

"I forgot to thank you for saving my life," I'd say.

Yeah, right.

I turned back towards the bush I'd hidden my bra in, but caught a glimpse of something moving on the path. Someone on the path, coming towards me—I recognized my mom. Panic set in, and without giving it any thought whatsoever, I jumped into the underbrush and forced my way through, hunkering down over a pile of malodorous pine needles and unidentifiable rotting vegetation. I plugged my nose and tried to breathe silently, even though my heart was hammering like crazy.

Mom walked by without even looking in my direction. I waited, moving only to slap at my face when I felt a tickle, scared now that I'd plunged into a den full of spiders. When I was sure Mom was gone, I stood up and brushed down my clothes, feeling ridiculous. I tried to find the bush with my bra, but somehow in my reckless rush to hide, I lost track of it.

I couldn't very well leave the bra. I only had two of them to my name after losing one in the creek, and if my undergarments kept disappearing, Mom was sure to notice. I batted ineffectually at branches, thinking surely the darned thing wasn't dingy enough to be camouflaged among the leaves.

"Looking for this?"

Fred.

I slowly turned. He held my bra out, dangling from a stick, his head cocked to one side as he patently appraised me. From the quizzical look on his face it appeared he'd already done the mental calculations necessary to determine that the bra in his hand would not, could not, possibly fit my chest.

"N-no," I stuttered.

His brows dropped. “Really.”

I lifted my chin and stepped out of the brush with as much dignity as I could muster. Explaining myself suddenly seemed impossible. Even if I came up with a plausible excuse for the bra, he still had some valid questions about yesterday’s big otter, my nakedness, and the General Lee clone.

I sighed and decided to pack it in. I’d only trudged about ten feet back the way I came when he said, “Hey! You can’t just leave.”

“Try and stop me,” I muttered.

“What?”

I heard his footsteps behind me on the path, but kept walking. He came up alongside me.

“So you’re just gonna go,” he said.

Frustrated, I stopped.

“What do you want me to say? I can’t explain anything to you.”

Technically, that wasn’t true. I could tell him I was a shapeshifter—show him, but instinctively I knew that would be a mistake. A big mistake. I remembered my mom’s face when she told me my father had shown her. She’d looked so devastated, said she’d freaked. And that’s exactly what Fred would do, what anyone would do under the circumstances.

“Why not?” He was pleading now.

“Because you wouldn’t understand.”

I started walking again, but this time he grabbed my arm.

“Don’t go. Look, you don’t have to tell me anything you don’t want to. Just…talk to me awhile, okay?”

I wanted to talk to him forever. But despite what he said, I knew I’d have to tell him something. I’d invented a name yesterday, but for the life of me I couldn’t remember what it was. It would be an awfully uncomfortable conversation with me not able to give him the smallest hint about myself. I needed to go home and concoct a plausible background for this person I was trying to be. I didn’t feel clever enough to wing it, and his nearness wasn’t helping matters.

I shook my head sadly. “I have to go. But…I’ll meet you here tomorrow. After school.”

As soon as I said it, I knew he would pounce. “You go to Ashworth?”

“No.” I had no idea what other schools were in the area. To stave off further questions, I reached out and snagged my bra off the stick he held.

“Don’t!” he tried to take it back from me, but I held it behind my back. Then he said, “It was lying in a patch of poison ivy branches.”

Another sigh escaped me, this one long and drawn out. “Of course it was.”

Chapter Fifteen

When I got home, I stuffed the bra in a grocery bag, tied it tight and shoved it under the bed before washing and rinsing my hands six or seven times in the bathroom sink. I'd taken care on the return trip not to forget and scratch my bare skin anywhere and spread the joy. If I had to be stuck being Titania Strauss, I didn't want to compound my unattractiveness by rubbing poison ivy into my eyes. Can we say, 'Quasimodo?' As it was, my hands were probably in for it—I wished I knew how soon.

I also wished, for about the millionth time, that I had a computer. I wanted to look up poison ivy to see what to expect. The evergreen bush I'd hidden my bra in had leaves, but it never occurred to me that the poison ivy rumored by Gina to be in the vicinity was in fact running rampant around the trunks of the bushes and trees—but hadn't yet sprouted. I hadn't seen any tell-tale tri-leaf configurations, therefore I couldn't very well have avoided them. That didn't mean the denuded branches from last year's crop couldn't still give me a rash.

I tried to find an encyclopedia in the condo with no luck. Gramma had some books, but they were mostly knitting patterns and large print romance novels. The only thing even close was a Scrabble dictionary—but I already knew how to spell poison and ivy and itch.

After a quick dinner of generic chicken noodle soup from a can, I got to work on my homework, but it only corralled a small portion of my attention. I'd always considered myself a pragmatic person, able to bounce back from adversity with relative composure, if not outright aplomb. We were poor; I was ugly. That was my reality. But I knew I couldn't avoid Mom, and my new reality, forever. On the outside, I was living life as per usual, sitting here doing my homework like nothing had changed. On the inside, barely contained, my mind was a whirling inferno of doubt. The Cataclysm may have altered the whole world, but what was happening to me now was so much closer to home.

Yet over and above all of that was the knowledge that at seventeen years-old, I had my first 'date' tomorrow. That it would be more of a clandestine meeting in the woods did nothing to take the gloss off. In fact, the secrecy gave it an added edge. I was excited and scared and realized I'd best knock out my homework so I could work on that background for the new me.

Mom called right before I went to bed. She didn't give me a hard time for dodging her again, but she did say, "It's really important that we talk, sweetie. Tomorrow is my day off, so plan on it, if not in the morning first thing, then right after school. Got it?"

Since I already had rather urgent after-school plans, I promised her I would be at the breakfast table with bells on.

In bed, my thoughts were all about Fred, how he'd said "Just…talk to me awhile," and looked at me like he couldn't tear his eyes away. It was true the girl he couldn't look away from was beautiful. Fred didn't know her; he was enamored of her looks. I tried to remind myself that not one of the attractive people in the world was responsible for their basic appearance. They could attempt to enhance that appearance all they wanted, but heredity provided the foundation. The important thing was that attractiveness wasn't limited to a person's looks; it's a package deal that includes intelligence, personality, morality.

Cinderella was blessed with good genes and had a fairy godmother to enhance her looks, but if she were dumb as a rock, or a flagrant slut, or her personality was as drab as her pre-magic duds, the prince probably would have looked elsewhere—eventually.

I had never flirted in my entire life. I hadn't even really fantasized about it—that was how sure I'd always been that I would never attract a boy. But I read a lot, living vicariously through the characters in my favorite novels. Maybe I could tap into that.

I finally fell asleep from mental exhaustion. No matter how many times I told myself I could pull this off, the fact that I would always be Titania Strauss on the inside begged to differ with me.

The alarm woke me way before I was ready. I lay there, clinging to the remnants of a dream that may or may not have had Fred in it, cursing the downstairs neighbors. Penny and her mother had had another knock-down-drag-out last night at the inconvenient hour of two a.m. There weren't enough pillows in the world to block out the sound of their shrieking. Altogether, I estimate I'd gotten about four hours sleep.

Mom was probably waiting at the table for me. Booyah.

I'd intended to take a quick shower, but the warm cascading water hypnotized my tapped-out brain. I think I actually dozed off standing there. When I finally got myself together enough to dry off, dress, and brush my hair, I expected Mom to be irritated.

But she wasn't there. Instead I heard some kind of commotion outside.

I stepped out onto the mat, shivering in the cold morning air. Gross Mr. Burns from across the way was looking out his window, as usual. I ignored him and walked barefoot to the rail.

The noises I'd heard came from a group of people, my mother included, standing by the side of the pool. Subdued sobs echoed from the corridor below. It sounded like Penny's mother. One of the men talking to my mom was a uniformed police officer. I was about to descend the stairs to ask Mom what was going on when I looked into the pool and saw her.

She was face up at the bottom of the pool. About an inch of greenish water covered her, but didn't conceal her body. Her eyes were open and her face was frozen in a look of terror.

Penny.

Chapter Sixteen

I wish I could say I'd never seen a dead body before, but I had. On the trip to Salt Lake City, we'd had to pass a horrific ten-car pileup outside of Twin Falls, Idaho. There was no ambulance service or paramedics present during the half hour it took us to drive around the mass of crumpled metal and bodies and debris. I tried not to look, but a horrified kind of fascination kept urging me to sneak glances. I know it was hard for Mom, a nurse, to ignore the dead and dying and keep inching forward. Several cars had stopped, but instead of helping out, they were siphoning gas from the wrecks and looting the victims. Mom knew we'd become a victims, too, if she tried to intervene. Her knuckles were white on the steering wheel as she whispered over and over, "There's nothing I can do for them. There's nothing I can do."

It didn't look like Mom and I were going to have our talk this morning. I went back inside and finished getting ready for school. After grabbing my backpack, I went back outside and this time, walked up to Mom.

She put her arms around me as soon as she saw me.

"What happened?" I asked.

"No one knows. I came home from work and found her there. It was too late."

I noticed Mom's pant legs were soaked. She must have gone into the pool to check for a pulse. Even if she'd wanted to, she wouldn't have been strong enough to haul Penny's body up the steep incline into the dry shallow end of the pool.

I didn't have to tell the police what I'd heard the night before because Mrs. Wharton, Penny's mother, was crying, "It's all my fault! She came home late last night and we had a fight. She stormed out and must have fallen…" her words trailed off as a renewed bout of sobbing overtook her. I felt tears of sympathy start in my own eyes.

"Go to school," Mom said and I nodded. With a final squeeze, she released me from the hug and gently shoved me away.

I didn't look at Penny again as I left the courtyard.

I was hoping to run into Gina on the way to school, but didn't see her or anyone else I knew. She was already in her seat when I got to English class. After Mr. Collins took roll, I felt a tap on my back. I turned and Gina slipped me a note.

I read it quickly, and while Mr. Collins was writing something on the blackboard, jotted a quick response and handed it back to her. A few minutes later, I felt the tap again. This time, I reached over my shoulder without turning, because Mr. Collins was facing the students and was in full-on lecture mode. Gina let go of the note before I closed my hand around it fully, and the folded piece of paper fluttered to the floor. My whole body stiffened up and it felt like my heart stopped.

"What's this?" Mr. Collins asked, striding along the narrow aisle between rows and snatching up the note before I got my wits about me.

I had never passed a note before in my life, nor had I ever been in trouble in school, not the slightest bit. I clenched my hands together to keep them from shaking.

"Well well," Mr. Collins said after he'd unfolded and perused the note. "Do you know what I do when students are caught passing notes in class?"

I happened to know exactly what he did, since I'd already plucked the answer out of his mind. I cringed away from the gleefully evil look he gave me.

He goose-stepped smartly to the front of the class and turned on his heels. Demonstrating his flair for the dramatic, he waved the paper through the air before settling his glasses on the tip of his nose.

"Ahem." It was more of an attention-getter than a true clearing of the throat, even though he already had everyone's rapt attention. He read, and I was horrified to hear his voice go up an octave as if he were trying to mimic us, "Tainie, I'm sorry I stood you up yesterday. Did you get any?"

The entire class burst out laughing. It took all my courage not to drop my forehead down on my desk. Great. I knew what I'd written, knew what was coming and prayed a black hole would open up and swallow me, or better yet, swallow Mr. Collins before he ruined my life. At least Jessica wasn't sitting in her seat; she'd apparently called in sick.

"And in response," Mr. Collins continued, "Miss Strauss replies, 'No, but it got me! Will explain later."

I didn't think it was possible for the class to laugh any more uproariously than they already had, but when Mr. Collins relayed Gina's final communication to me, "Want to get some after school?" they broke out into hysterics.

One kid actually stood up and wrapped his arms around himself, pantomiming a passionate embrace.

"Sit down, Martin! Alright, class, that's enough." Mr. Collins sounded gruff now, as if Martin's antics made him suddenly realize how his students had interpreted our note. He picked up a yardstick and whapped his desk with it several times. "That's enough!"

He'd riled them all up and now couldn't regain control. Served him right, but the sooner he got the upper hand, the better for me and poor Gina. I slumped down in my seat and refused to look up from the surface of my desk. I listened for Fred's voice among the guffaws, but couldn't make out whether he'd joined in.

Of course he did. If this had happened to someone else, even I'd be laughing.

The class did finally settle down and Mr. Collins approached me for the final humiliation. He dropped the note on my desk and said, "Passing notes in my class is an automatic detention, but in this case, I'll take pity on you girls and defer punishment since I suspect you will never commit this particular infraction again. Am I correct in that assumption?"

I nodded miserably, thinking, *this is your version of pity*?

Mr. Collins spent the rest of the hour in an ebullient mood. I wouldn't have pegged him for a sadist, but to all appearances he was basking in the glow of his triumphant moment. Maybe it was simply because he'd gotten an overwhelming response from his usually bored class. Or maybe he thought he'd been clever, catching us passing a note, as if half the class didn't text each other when he wasn't looking. Either way, I would be more wary of him in future.

He didn't try to speak to me or Gina at the end of class, and Gina was out the door first, as usual. I didn't see her again until lunch hour. I'd decided to head home in the hopes that Mom was awake and we could get that talk out of the way so it didn't interfere with my after-school plans. Those plans had almost gotten nixed by the note fiasco—if what Mr. Collins said was true, we'd barely avoided detention. If given the choice between the two, detention or getting humiliated, I probably would have willingly chosen the embarrassment.

I would do anything to see that look in Fred's eyes again.

Gina caught up with me a block away from school. I expected her to apologize for getting me in trouble yet again, but all she did was rant about Mr. Collins.

"He's such a big jerk-face! Can you believe he did that? What kind of a teacher is he? We should report him or something."

"For what? Maybe we got off lucky."

"Lucky? Are you crazy? I can't believe you're not mad."

I shrugged, but Gina didn't let it go.

"It seriously doesn't bother you that he made us sound like we were…"

Gina couldn't even say it.

"Gay? It's no big deal. Our high school careers will be over in two years. Once we're out, we're free to walk away from whatever reputation we were saddled with—deserved or otherwise. It's a big world. I for one don't plan on hanging around this town."

Gina looked at me like I'd grown a second head, and for a moment I wondered if I could do it. I suppressed a grin, but she saw and misinterpreted it.

"So you buy into that crap?" she asked. "Adults force-feed us this 'life doesn't start until after school' malarkey and you believe it?"

I snorted. "Do the math. We get to live, like, eighty years if we're lucky. The first eighteen is enforced education, twenty-two if you go to college. That leaves us with about sixty years of freedom—if you don't count the dead-end job, assuming you end up with one. That's plenty of time to build yourself a new rep."

Gina sighed, but it didn't signal capitulation. "That's all fine and dandy, but Mr. Collins shouldn't be allowed to mess up a kid's rep in the first place."

We'd reached the corner where Gina would split off if she were to go to her house. I stopped because I didn't want her to come home with me.

"I'm sure he didn't realize how the note would sound," I said. "Heck, we wrote it and didn't realize how it would sound. There's worse things people could think about us, you know."

"Like what?"

I thought about all the names I'd been called in my lifetime. If I wanted, I could recite the more hurtful ones, the ones that stuck in my psyche like burrs. Then she'd know how awful things had really been for me. But underneath the bluster, she looked fragile. She wanted to believe things would get better for her. After years of listening to my highly persuasive mother, I was just the person to convince her life after geekdom was possible.

But I knew she'd be a hard sell and I didn't have time to take that chore on at the moment.

"Like a lot of things. Listen, I gotta get home. My mom wants to have a talk. But I was thinking it might not be a great idea after all to get Jessica with poison ivy."

"Why not? She wasn't here today, so that's a victory right there."

"Yeah, it looks like we got away with it—once—but you can't put off the inevitable forever."

Gina took a step back, looking betrayed. "Oh, wow, that's it then. Thanks for nothing."

"Don't be like that," I said hastily. "We'll think of something, okay? Something legal that doesn't require repeatedly sending her to the emergency room."

"Whatever." She walked off and I let her. I valued our budding friendship, but really, she was so touchy, so sensitive. It was exhausting.

Chapter Seventeen

The pool area was roped off with yellow 'Crime Scene' tape. I had to go the long way around, past Mrs. Zimmerman's door. She must have just been outside because the air smelled like cigarette smoke. I saw a smoldering butt in one of her neighbors' flower pots and wondered if she thought they wouldn't notice.

From behind me, I heard a door open and Mrs. Z's raspy voice called, "Hey!"

Warily, I turned. She held a hand up for me to wait and disappeared back inside her house. In a moment she returned with an armful of pink clothes, which she proceeded to shove at me.

"Tell your mom I'm sorry. It's this damned Cataclysm air; makes people crazy. But I don't need no trouble." Under wrinkled, droopy lids, her eyes cut to the swimming pool, which only hours before held Penny's lifeless body.

I hadn't forgotten what I'd done to Mrs. Z, who had probably come to the obvious conclusion that she'd hallucinated her naked self entering the laundry room. But 'Penny' had been the only one inside when Mrs. Z investigated. I had no idea if Mrs. Z followed up later and confronted her.

But I could find out.

She obliged me by glaring into my face as if she couldn't understand why I was still standing there. I asked, "Did you have anything to do with what happened to Penny?"

Mrs. Z's head snapped back on her neck, and her affronted expression mirrored her thoughts.

"What are you, some kind of nosy junior detective? Get outta here before I change my mind."

I left before she could tell me twice, but I'd gotten my answer. Mrs. Z may be a vicious old hag, but she didn't do it and she didn't know who had.

In the condo, a surprise waited for me. Mom had a visitor.

"Oh, honey," she exclaimed when she saw me. "I'm so glad you came home for lunch! You remember Seamus."

He looked different dressed casually in a sweatshirt and jeans rather than the flamboyant pirate coat. His hair was shorter; almost a military cut, and his blue eyes looked funny, like the irises were swirling, or the contrasting lights and darks within were clashing with each other in some kind of optical illusion. It was an eerie effect that inexplicably made me flash back to being on the ocean. I fought a sudden wave of nausea and dropped my eyes.

"Hi," I said.

"I see Martha came to her senses," Mom remarked as I dropped the clothes on the couch.

"She said she was sorry. Blamed it on the Cataclysm."

Mom gave a short laugh. "Don't we all."

"It would be more accurate to blame it on the Gossamer Sphere," Seamus said in his rich, deep voice.

I felt that old irritation surface and tried to squelch it as I went to open the refrigerator. I didn't know what it would take for me to stop doubting.

Nothing in the fridge looked good, even though I'd been starving a few minutes ago.

"The Gossamer Sphere," I said. "Asteroid, right?"

"More than a mere asteroid," Seamus replied. "It is now part of this planet, controlling our magnetic field. We discovered much about it and its purpose during the Cataclysm."

"Here." Mom jumped up and pulled open the pantry door. "You sit and chat with Uncle Seamus. I'll make you a sandwich. How much time do you have?"

I glanced at the clock. "About ten minutes."

Seamus pursed his lips and said, "I'd best talk fast, then."

I sat. "Are you really my uncle? I mean, are you my father's brother?"

"No. I'm not sure who your father was. I am your mother's grandmother's brother."

My great-grandmother Nora had died well before I was born. Seamus didn't look to be a day over twenty-five. "Oh, so…" I gestured to his face. "That's not really…you?"

He looked at my mom, whose back was to us, but who had frozen in place with her arm extended towards the loaf of bread on the counter.

"How much does she know?" He sounded slightly annoyed.

Mom's shoulders slumped and she sighed. Without turning, she said,

"She wouldn't listen."

Seamus frowned, and to prevent him from criticizing Mom, I jumped in. "It's true. I never believed a thing she tried to tell me. Even now I find it all hard to—absorb."

He turned those spooky eyes on me again and just as I realized what he was doing, he smiled.

"Yes," he said. "When you read someone's thoughts, they may notice your eyes look strange, so take care."

"How do we do it? Mom said it wasn't magic."

He shrugged. "It's not. It's a brainwave thing. Caitlin's the scientist, she'd be able to explain it better, but she's dug in like a tick somewhere; significantly harder to find than me."

"You're in hiding?"

"Always. There aren't many of us, and there are those who would like to see us obliterated."

I shivered a little, more at his tone, so cold and flat, than the words. "But…you stopped the Cataclysm, right? Nobody knows?"

Seamus shook his head slowly. "In order to convince the public of our role in stopping the Gossamer Sphere, we would first have to show them what we are, and that we cannot do. That is your first lesson. No matter how much you may want to confess to your friends that you are different, take heed. Friends can easily turn into enemies, especially if they consider you a threat."

Up until this very moment, it had all been more of a game to me than anything else. An impossible, horrible, wonderful game.

"What do I need to know?"

He ticked the items off on his fingers. "One: after surviving initiation sickness, which you already have, you will never be ill again. Two: you cannot die from natural causes, but you can be killed. Three: mind-reading is limited by distance, and most of us have to look directly into our target's eyes. Four: there is an ancient society that call themselves the Guild that you must steer clear of at all cost. They will torture and kill you to obtain knowledge about us. Which brings me to number five: avoid iron."

I skipped right over the incomprehensible 'torture and kill' part and asked, "Avoiding iron is kind of hard to do, isn't it? I mean, I used to have to take supplements. I've been anemic my whole life."

"Caitlin suspects that all the descendants who survive initiation are. The crown you touched was made from the same substance the gossamer sphere consisted of. Caitlin is the scientist; she'd be able to satisfy your curiosity further, but for the time being, know that you don't need to avoid foods that have iron in them, just don't consume it in a vitamin, or wear it against your skin in jewelry. Exposure to iron alone will make you sick and strip you of your abilities for the duration of your contact with it—and the guild knows it. Their favorite trick was to clap us in irons."

I finally took a moment to contemplate this Guild, and all I could think was: Is he freaking kidding me? There's a Guild of crazy people out there that wanted us all dead?

I felt Mom's hand on my shoulder. She held out my sandwich and I took it numbly.

"You're scaring the crap out of her, Seamus."

"Good. I forgot one thing: don't try to change into something that was never alive. You may become anything your DNA recognizes, warm-blooded air-breathers only, including animals that we did not directly evolve from, within the scope of your size. Do not attempt to become, say, a mosquito."

"Would that hurt or kill me?"

He laughed. "No. If you are not running for your life, it will merely inconvenience you because you will fail. If, however, you need to change quickly, choose something that you are familiar with."

So that's why I couldn't become a fish. I thought of General Lee, and vowed to practice shifting into something less hairy and slobbery.

"You have already shifted." It was a statement, and I saw that his eyes were weird again. It bothered me.

"Do you make it a habit to read people?" I didn't try to hide my testiness.

His eyebrows rose. "Yes. Why wouldn't I?"

"I don't know, maybe to avoid offending them?"

He laughed again. It was a merry sound in direct contrast to his earlier coldness. "As I've said, there are very few who realize I have the capability. Now, it seems our ten minutes are nearly up. Do you have any final questions for me? I have a flight out this evening and as your mother can attest, I'm not easy to find, so your idle questions will have to wait."

I had about a million questions, but a few burned more brightly than the rest.

"You don't know who my father was?"

He looked down at the table. "Not for certain. There was one of the folk, recently deceased, who had his own agenda. He had twisted notions about bringing back the glory days. It seems he may have sought out descendants of the folk and tricked them into bearing his progeny."

Mom said, "When the Cataclysm started, Seamus put up a website designed to bring the folk out of hiding to stop the Gossamer Sphere. That's how I found him. I knew you were one of them, Tainie. It was a surprise to discover I was, too."

"My sister," Seamus said, "was the last child my mother bore before the Guild caught up to her in Paris during World War I. Nora never had the opportunity to touch the crown. She lived a normal life-span and to protect herself, never spoke of whence she came. There are many descendants of the folk who do not know who they are. If your mother had known, she might have recognized what your father was trying to do." He pressed his lips together and sent an apologetic look Mom's way.

"It wasn't anyone's fault," she said. Her face softened and she squeezed my shoulder. "I wouldn't change any of it for the world. No one could have known he would target me like that. Brian was a—rogue—I guess is the word. Living as long as he did, watching everyone he loved die, I imagine he went a little crazy."

"I'm just as old," Seamus said shortly, as if he had no patience with that excuse. He looked at me. "There is a price to being what you are. Our children die at birth—most of them. Of those who survive, the ones with the purest blood, that is, whose father and mother are both of the folk, are most likely to survive initiation, should they choose to attempt it. Although the crown is hidden again, of course, so that cannot happen. Your initiation was a fluke, and it's a miracle you survived."

He didn't have to tell me. I'd been so sick from that lovely 'initiation sickness' there were times I recall praying for death.

"How old are you?" I asked, suddenly dreading the answer.

His jaw jutted forward a bit and he gave a little grunt. Those assessing blue eyes watched for my reaction. "I would have to do some calculations, but I believe I'm nearing the 2,000 mark. To answer your next question, I stopped celebrating my birthday centuries ago."

I could tell that was an old joke with him, but I didn't find it amusing. I think my heart may have actually stopped beating for a second as the implications began to sink in. I'm pretty sure what he did next was to prevent me from freaking out, although technically, it backfired. He stood.

"One more thing. Watch your limbs. You're a tiny little thing. Can't afford to lose body mass. Take me for instance..." He shifted, but very little changed. He grew a few inches in height as his left arm disappeared, leaving an empty sleeve up to the shoulder. "I used to be taller, but had to borrow mass to create a new arm."

Horrified, I glanced at Mom and the surprise on her face told me she hadn't known.

"Seamus! You are not reassuring her," she said.

He smiled, but it held no humor. "Why would I? There is a reason we stopped allowing initiates to touch the crown, you know. Titania will be the last."

Chapter Eighteen

If my teachers strapped me into a highchair and spoon-fed me my lessons, I still would have failed any and all quizzes on the material that day. It was one thing to find out that an ancient society of psychos got their kicks out of torturing and killing us; and another thing altogether to discover that violent death was the *only* way to kill us. Mom had forgiven my father because she empathized with his plight. Like he had some kind of survivor syndrome that affected his sanity, but to her it was understandable because of course living forever would rob you of that sanity.

By the time Chemistry finally rolled around, I had a headache, which was supposed to be impossible if Seamus was to be believed. We didn't get sick.

I sat on my stool and examined my hands. There was no sign of trauma, not the faintest blemish to indicate the poison ivy had taken hold.

Gina gave me a little wave when she came in, but kind of surreptitiously, like she didn't want anyone to see and assume we were exchanging a lover's greeting. Fred hardly said a word to me all through class. He kept pulling his cell out of his pocket when Mr. Applebee wasn't looking and texting someone.

At the end of the day, our youngish but stern-faced principal, Mrs. Voorhees, came on the loudspeaker.

"The faculty and I here at Ashworth Academy are saddened to confirm the death of one of our alumni, Penny Wharton. Penny graduated two years ago and was a member of the student body and captain of the cheerleading squad. She was an exemplary student and will be deeply missed. We ask that rumors surrounding the cause of death be kept to a minimum. At this time, I understand police have no reason to believe it was anything other than a tragic accident. A memorial service is in the works and will be announced soon. Please refrain from contacting Mrs. Wharton, who asks that her privacy be respected in this, the most difficult of times. Thank you."

Mr. Applebee interrupted the low murmuring that broke out all over class by telling us, “I had her in her junior year. She was a good kid. Did any of you know her?”

Not one person raised their hand. Fred glanced up from his texting, but didn’t say a word, and I knew he knew Penny. I’d seen him get into that blue Mustang with her in the passenger seat just yesterday.

Maybe he didn’t feel like talking about it. He had been distracted all afternoon.

Or maybe he knew something and didn’t feel like implicating himself. Either way, I hardly cared. All I could think about was seeing him later in the woods, as Tory. I’d remembered the name I invented and was ready with a plausible background, should it be needed. My hope was that there wouldn’t be much talking.

After class, Gina approached me in the hall.

“Come here.” She spoke in an undertone. I raised my eyebrows but followed her to a large glass-fronted trophy case mounted on the wall in the main hallway. A bunch of kids, mostly girls who looked like they could be cheerleaders, were hanging around. A few were crying.

Gina managed to get close enough to point out a photograph in the case. “Recognize the girl in front?” she asked quietly.

I nodded. It was Penny.

Gina grabbed my arm and dragged me out of earshot of the cheerleader types. “I saw her yesterday! I don’t know if you noticed because you were busy fetching your shoe out of the gutter, but that car Fred got into? She was in it, I swear!”

“I know. She lives in the condo below me.”

Gina’s excitement deflated like a balloon. “When were you gonna tell me?”

“I saw her body this morning, Gina. It wasn’t something I felt like gossiping about.”

“Oh, my God. That’s awful. What did she look like?”

I started walking toward the exit and shot her a look that told her without words what I thought of that question.

“I’m sorry,” she said, scrambling to keep up. “I know it’s morbid, but I want to be a pathologist when I grow up. Stuff like that fascinates me. Where was she? I heard she drowned.”

Unbidden, my mind conjured an image of Penny’s face under the brackish water. Did drowning victims look horrified?

“Maybe. But if she did, it was because she hit her head on the side of the pool or something. There wasn’t enough water.”

“She was in the pool? Did it look like someone pushed her? I mean, did you notice Fred didn't admit he knew her?"

We'd reached the courtyard, and I stopped next to the fountain. "It didn't look like anything! She was just—dead, okay?"

I strode off, angry that Gina seemed to want to implicate Fred with no evidence whatsoever. I wasn't sure what she had against him, why she was always willing to believe the worst of him, but it was getting old.

She quickly caught up with me. "Sorry again! I get it that you're traumatized or whatever. But you know who was driving that mustang?"

I didn't know, and I'd wondered, but I also didn't want to encourage Gina to keep talking about it. She told me anyway.

"It was Fred's big brother, Steve. Steve Spencer? Heard of him?"

She said it like I should have. "Only because my mom works for his mom."

"Wow, really? They're, like, rich. Steve's some kind of badass golf prodigy. I'll bet you a million bucks he dated Penny when he went to Ashworth."

It was the first thing she said that I agreed with. It did seem likely that Stephen Spencer and Penny Wharton had history. It occurred to me that Fred and his brother may have been among the last to see Penny alive, information the police had probably already discovered.

Which meant if the cops wanted to question him, Fred might not make our date. That sunk me into a pensive mood for the next two blocks. I pretended to listen to Gina blather all the way to the corner where she normally split off for her house.

"So this is it," she said, pushing her glasses up on her nose and flashing a tight little smile. "If you don't see me tomorrow I'll probably be in an alley somewhere getting my butt kicked by Jessica and her crew. Unless you have any more bright ideas on how to delay it?"

I gave her a regretful look. "I'm fresh out. Except…you could talk to your counselor or Mr. Applebee, you know."

She made a scoffing sound, but replied, "I just might."

With a jaunty wave, she skipped out into the crosswalk while humming the funeral dirge.

Inside the condo, I expected Mom to want to talk some more, so I'd invented another mythical study session with a friend and was prepared to spring it on her.

Instead of talk, Mom wanted answers. She held up the black garbage bag with Gramma's coat in it and demanded, "What's this?"

"Ohhhh," I said. "Yeah, that."

"We can't afford to have this dry-cleaned, you know."

"I know! It—It got wet the other night when you made me walk to work with you. Remember how hard it was raining?"

She rolled her eyes. "And you put it in a garbage bag instead of hanging it up to dry? What were you thinking? Now it smells funny. It's probably all moldy."

I was just glad she bought my story. "Gramma has some Woolite in the cupboard. Can we wash it by hand?"

"*We* are not going to do anything. You can wash it right this instant, young lady."

Gramma Foster was sitting in her lounge chair softly snoring. I was glad she'd missed the exchange.

I'd never been one to rebel outright against anything Mom required of me, but for once, I felt like balking. It just seemed wrong somehow that a mind-reading, shapeshifting immortal should have to get her hands dirty doing menial chores. But I obediently took the bag into the bathroom and dumped the coat into the tub. It got a cursory wash and rinse at best, before I hung it from the curtain rod on a thick plastic hanger. Then I slipped into the room I shared with Mom to change.

I'd already decided on an outfit. My post-Cataclysm wardrobe was limited and I had to be careful Tory didn't wear something Tainie had already been seen in. Not that my clothing was all that memorable, but I'd seen Fred's eyes drift down to my chest on more than one occasion. He was probably thinking more about the inconsistency between my face and bod rather than taking note of my attire, but I couldn't chance it. Since Tory was taller and thinner than me, I chose the only clothes that would fit properly once I shifted: a pair of old stretch jeans Mom had grown out of and yesterday's black sweater. I would also be forced to wear Mom's old work shoes again.

I hoped Tory's beautiful face and willowy figure would distract Fred from her lame duds.

When I told Mom I had to study at Gina's house, she said, "Again? Well, I need her phone number then."

I didn't happen to have it. "I'll call you when I get there, okay?" I knew she'd be mad when I 'forgot' to do so, but I didn't have much choice. If I called from a payphone or anywhere else, Gramma Foster's phone would store the number in its memory.

Mom looked doubtful, but she said, "Alright, honey, if you're sure you don't want to hang out and talk some more…"

"I'm all talked out, to be honest." I offered her a smile to take the sting out of the statement. Then I hit her with something I knew would sway her. "It's all so overwhelming, you know? I just want to focus on being a kid for the time being."

Guilt washed over me as tears formed in her eyes.

"I understand," she said with a sniff. "Go. Study. I'm glad you have a friend."

"Me, too." I reached for the doorknob, but she stopped me.

"Don't you need your backpack? And it's freezing out there. The radio said it might get cold enough to snow. Wear my coat."

She bustled to the utility closet and pulled out her knee-length black overcoat. She held it open for me to slip into, then she turned me around to fasten the buttons. I rolled my eyes.

"I can button my own buttons, Mom."

She brushed a hand down my front to wipe away invisible dust. "I know."

She was getting maudlin, so I decided to make my escape. "I'll be home before ten."

"That late?"

"*Before* ten. I don't think it will take that long, but we have a Chemistry quiz tomorrow."

Luckily, I got out of there without having to take my backpack, which Fred would certainly recognize as Tainie's.

As soon as I started down the steps, my heart began pounding in anticipation of seeing him. I shoved my hands in Mom's pockets to stop them from shaking. By the time I got to the park, I felt like I was on the verge of an anxiety attack. Profuse nervous perspiration would not impress him, especially if Tory stunk to high heaven. Eau de B.O. was no one's parfum of choice.

As planned, Tainie ducked into the brick building housing the park's restroom and came out as Tory. There was no one close enough to notice the two very different girls had identical outfits.

A strange thing happened as I neared the woods. My heart and breathing settled down and my hands became steady. Tory, with her huge eyes that had lashes so thick she didn't need mascara, and whose skin was so fine she didn't need makeup, had no reason whatsoever to be uneasy.

He was sitting on 'his' rock by the creek.

Chapter Nineteen

Somehow, my lifelong clumsiness did not assert itself over Tory's body, which was lithe and fit. The water had long since receded after the storm, and the flat-topped boulders embedded as the path across the creek were dry. I jumped from rock to rock with the grace of a ballerina. Or so I hoped.

I stopped on the bank several feet from Fred. He'd slid off his rock and was now leaning against it, one ankle crossed over the other, casual and suave. He still wore his jeans and school jacket. The afternoon light hadn't yet begun to fade, but the lowering sun produced a thick, dappled shade. The wind had picked up and it riffled his short hair. My nose and ears were cold, but I had plenty of heat in my cheeks.

The first thing he said was, "I didn't think you'd come."

"I said I would."

He shrugged carelessly and a small, crooked smile appeared on his lips. I was dying to know what was going through his mind, so I peeked.

He was happy to see me. I looked beautiful. Then suddenly, he noticed something weird and strangely familiar about my eyes.

Alarmed, I jerked my gaze away from his and stumbled backward.

"What's wrong?" He strode forward and put his hands out to steady me. "Are you alright?"

I forced a little laugh. "Fine. Fine. Just a bit dizzy. I skipped lunch."

Technically, it was true. I'd only taken a few bites of the sandwich Mom made me. But I didn't want to think about any of that now.

Fred guided me to his rock. The only warning I got before he lifted me bodily onto it was, "Alley-oop!"

"Thanks." The rock had a natural depression in the center, but I had to tuck one foot under my butt and sit on it in an effort to get comfortable. At least I was beginning to feel comfortable in his presence. Well, as comfortable as a girl can get when she's fighting the constant urge to jump into his arms and wrap her legs around him.

“So…” he said. “What do you want to talk about? Because I can talk about anything. Almost anything. Basketball, Legos, Nascar, astronomy, dogs, um, golf…”

“Legos?”

He smiled. “I’ve outgrown them, but I still have a working knowledge. My dad used to put them together with me. He had a thing for the Star Wars sets.”

“Ah, so you’re a closet nerd?”

“Nah,” he shoved his hands in the pockets of his jeans. “I’m a blatant nerd. Have you not picked up on my dorkismo?”

I knew he was smart, if a little on the sly side. He’d been willing to help Gina and I get back at Jessica, so I also suspected he had a perverse sense of humor. Tory was more likely to receive the full measure of his charm, something Tainie had only guessed at. “Is that what they’re calling it now?”

He kicked at the dirt in an ‘aw garsh’ gesture. “My dad was a rock climber, a sky-diver, and he ran the New York Marathon twice. He was also an astronomer, which is about the nerdiest profession on the planet. But he never apologized for it…never worried about what people thought of him. He was a macho dork.”

I already knew, but I asked, “Was?”

“Yeah. My parents were broadsided by a cement mixer. The driver was trying to find the construction site and was talking to his boss on his cell phone. Dad was killed instantly and Mom ended up with a spinal cord injury, so she’s in a wheelchair. Nice, huh?”

“I’m sorry.” I was horrible at the sympathy thing. I never knew what to say; as if anything I could say would help or be of any comfort. I hoped my face told him how I felt.

“Well, that’s why you didn’t meet her. She doesn’t get around much. Mrs. Strauss, the lady who got the towels for us, is her nurse. She was worried about you when you just disappeared.”

“Your grandparents were talking about calling the police. Apparently they thought I was some kind of tramp looking for someone named Stephen.”

“My brother. Yeah, sorry about that. The grand ’rents are…” he trailed off and shrugged, as if they defied description.

I shifted position on the rock. “We can’t help who our family is.”

“True. You want to come over to my house? I ask because I can offer you a snack and a real chair with cushions instead of a pointy rock. I promise no one will accuse you of trying to seduce me for my money.”

“Good, because when I seduce someone, it’s because I really like them.” As soon as I said it, I felt a wave of heat suffuse my face, which, if he noticed it, would take the punch out of my first ever attempt at being risqué.

He noticed.

But it was okay because it made him lean close and reach up to place both hands gently on my cheeks. “Mind if I warm my hands? You’ve got quite the fire blazing.”

I laughed and inclined my head toward him. His mouth was only inches away from mine. Short of initiating contact myself, I was now employing every wile I had, through the subtly suggestive language of my body, to get him to make his move.

Instead, his brow wrinkled and he pulled back a bit. “Your laugh…your eyes...” he removed his hands from my cheeks and grasped the lapels of Mom’s coat, pulling me towards him, but only to inhale the scent rising off of me. Mom’s signature scent—a blend of jasmine and vanilla. “Even your perfume is so familiar.”

He looked baffled as his eyes roamed over my face. “Do I *know* you?”

As if his nearness hadn’t already raised my pulse, the shot of adrenaline that flooded my system sent it skyrocketing. I had two choices: I could run away and never see him as Tory again, thereby eliminating the risk that he might figure out who and what I was; or I could distract him. Distraction was by far the more palatable choice.

I wet my lips and in a husky voice asked, “Do you want to know me?”

I heard his indrawn breath and saw his eyes drop to my lips a fraction of a second before he kissed me. It was a gentle touch of his closed lips to mine, but still, it was enough to set my body afire with longing. The second kiss lasted longer as he slowly coaxed me to part my lips. I wanted so much for him to stop teasing and pull me into his arms. And then he did, sliding his hands around my back. I melted against his chest, my mouth fused to his, unable to catch my breath. He tore his lips from mine and I arched my back as he planted burning little kisses all down my neck. I was on the verge of hitching my hips forward so I could wrap my legs around him like I’d imagined doing earlier, when he murmured, “Mrs. Strauss.”

My eyes shot open wide as he pulled away. “What?”

“Your perfume. You smell like my mom’s nurse.”

Time for some quick bluffing. “So? It’s a popular scent.”

“Tory, I heard her talking to my mom. She has it made at some kind of apothecary in Ireland.” He ran his fingers over the smooth material of Mom’s coat. “This is hers, isn’t it? You stole it when you ran out of my house."

I was so relieved that his rationale was miles from the truth ("No, I was wearing *General Lee's* coat when I made my escape") that I immediately nodded. "Yes. I had no choice. I was scared your grandparents were going to have me arrested."

He planted a quick, hard, forgiving kiss on my lips and began unbuttoning the coat.

"Wha—what are you doing?" I stuttered.

He eased the coat off one side, pulling my sweater down with it and exposing my shoulder, which he then kissed. I fought luxurious shivers and protested, "It's a little cold out."

He kissed me again, on the lips, but didn't stop removing the coat. For a moment, I pretended he was stripping me for real and got lost in the fantasy. But when he got the coat off, he set it behind me on the rock and quickly pulled his school jacket off.

"Here. Take this, and I'll give Mrs. Strauss her coat back."

Obediently, I let him wrap me in the oversized jacket, which was warm from his body and smelled deliciously like Fred.

He stepped back and admired me, saying, "This isn't going to cause problems at your school, is it?"

I shook my head, surprised that he thought I'd even wear it to school. I may be inexperienced at this sort of thing, but I knew how it generally went—giving a girl your school jacket meant commitment. Fred was either moving pretty darn fast, didn't realize what he'd said, or was simply hoping I'd tell him where I went to school and didn't realize what he'd said. Little did he know I wouldn't be wearing it farther than the bathroom at the park.

It was becoming painfully clear that the need to clothe oneself properly would be a major disadvantage to being a shapeshifter.

Fred had just reached for me again when his cell phone rang. He sighed and said, "I'm sorry, I have to check this."

After tapping the screen looking at the display, he shot me an apologetic look and took the call. He walked several feet away, but I heard him say, "What's up?" After a moment, he said, "It's not a good time, bro." Then, "I know, but I can't right now." A long pause was followed by, "Fine. I'll be right there."

He discontinued the call and swore softly before turning to me with a regretful smile.

"Gotta go?" I tried to keep my voice light even though my disappointment was epic.

"Yeah." He put his arms around me and nuzzled my neck until I giggled.

"What's so important?" I asked.

He let out a low, frustrated growl. "My brother. He's…in trouble again."

I was so relaxed and at home in his arms that it slipped out: "Penny?"

He went as still as a statue for a second, then pulled away to stare at me, uncomprehending. "How did you know?"

I would have gladly traded my shapeshifting ability for a good time machine right about then.

"Because…I—I saw you yesterday. Um, in a blue car with, you know, Penny. She lives…lived…near me." It was the truth, but I'd managed to make it sound like a lie. By some miracle, he bought it.

"Oh. Yeah, well…" he turned his head away and continued almost to himself, "A lot of people probably saw us."

Emboldened, I took his chin in my hand and made him look at me. "Did something happen?"

"No! No, I swear, she was alive and—well, not happy exactly—when we dropped her off. Steve had nothing to do with it."

I didn't care if he noticed my weird eyes, I read his mind and found to my relief that he was telling the truth. But my relief was short-lived. Floating in his consciousness was an image that I, too, had seen—that of Penny lying face-up at the bottom of the pool. In his mind, however, it wasn't morning as it had been when the emergency personnel had arrived.

Fred had seen Penny's body in the dark of the night and hadn't notified anyone.

Chapter Twenty

I'd been gone only an hour, which turned out to be a good thing, because Gramma Foster was the only one home. I came inside clutching Fred's balled-up jacket, and she didn't even glance away from the television.

"Your mother's gone to the grocery store. I hope she remembers my ice cream."

I didn't bother reminding her that ice cream was scarce, and the fact that there was never any in the house had nothing to do with Mom forgetting to purchase it.

In the bedroom, I looked around for a place to stash Fred's coat and finally settled on stuffing it way under the bed.

It was bad enough I was going to have to lie to mom again and tell her I forgot her coat at Gina's house, but if Mom saw Fred's jacket, she might recognize it—as Fred had recognized hers. I sat on the bed and rubbed my temples. It didn't really matter; the lie wouldn't hold up very long anyway. As soon as Fred gave Mom her coat, the jig would be up. No way she wouldn't figure out my involvement then.

I laughed and said to myself, "And I would have gotten away with it, too, if it hadn't have been for the cold weather."

Blame it on the Cataclysm.

When Mom got home, she took off her windbreaker and hung it in the hall closet, thankfully not noticing the empty hanger where her coat should be. I helped her put away the groceries, two sacks of nutrient-poor, inexpensive staples.

"Did you have dinner yet?" she asked.

Before I could answer, the doorbell rang. I had a flash of panic that Fred decided to hand-deliver Mom's coat, but there were two strange men standing on the threshold.

"I'm Detective Roach of the Philadelphia P.D. and this is Detective Spivey. We're sorry to disturb you, ma'am, but we have a few questions regarding the death of your downstairs neighbor."

Mom peered at the badge the older, taller of the two held up and then invited them in.

Detective Roach's graying brown hair had receded about an inch from his forehead, but from the inquisitive tilt of Mom's head, I could tell he fit within the parameters of her version of handsome. He led his partner inside and Mom directed them to the kitchen table.

"Who's that? What's going on?" Gramma called in a querulous voice.

"It's detectives, Edna," Mom said loudly. "They're here about Penny."

"A Penny? What about a Penny?" Gramma asked.

I rolled my eyes at the younger detective, a short, stocky man with a too-tight suit. He didn't appear amused.

Mom went into the living room to explain recent events to Gramma Foster while the detectives sat. Since Gramma Foster had only the two chairs, I stood nearby.

"You must be…" Roach glanced at me and inspected his notepad. "Titania. Is that right?"

I nodded and blurted, "Do you know who killed Penny?"

Roach's left eyebrow shot up. "What makes you think she was killed?"

I looked into his eyes and his mind. They definitely thought it was murder. But, as he'd implied, I had no reason to jump to that conclusion.

I tried to look innocent as I responded, "I guess I didn't think you'd be here if it were an accident."

"Really. Are you saying you have information we should know about?"

I was in no way saying that. The question must be a standard 'trick them into revealing something' kind of question, but it did make me think about Fred, how he'd seen Penny's body hours before it had been reported.

"No," I said, hearing the resentment in my tone and hating it.

Roach treated me to a measuring stare as Mom came into the kitchen and asked, "Can I get you gentlemen some water? I'd offer coffee or tea, but…you know."

Everyone knew. If coffee was worth more than gold, tea was the new silver, without the pot.

"No thank you, Mrs. Strauss," Roach said. His ran his eyes over my pretty mom in a manner completely different from the way he'd just looked at me. It set my teeth on edge.

Spivey cleared his throat. "We wanted to ask you both a few

questions, obviously."

"We'd be happy to help in any way," Mom replied.

Roach consulted his notes and looked at her. "You were the first responder."

She nodded. "I saw her in the pool from the top of the stairwell and ran down. Right away I could see she'd been gone for some time, but I went in to check anyway."

"You're an R.N.?"

"No, Licensed Practical Nurse. I do private home health care."

"You work for the Spencer family?" Roach asked.

"Yes."

"Are you acquainted with Stephen Spencer?"

Mom looked slightly puzzled. "I met him a few times."

Roach nodded thoughtfully. Then he pinned me with a hard look. "We found a bag in the complex laundry room that contained some of Penny's clothing, and a note."

I stopped breathing, and Roach showed his teeth in a feral smile. His voice dropped. "Do you have anything you'd like to tell us, Titania?"

"What?" Mom asked. Her eyes darted from Roach to Spivey to me. "What do you mean?"

My fingerprints would be all over the bag I'd put Penny's clothing in as well as on the note that accompanied it. Roach was trying to trick me again. He'd successfully triggered my guilt reflex, but not for the reasons he was trying to uncover. I mentally tamped down the panic and tried to think what excuse to offer. As with Fred earlier, I went with a modified version of the truth.

"It's no big deal. She must have left some of her stuff in the washer or dryer and I didn't notice until I was folding clothes. I recognized the shirt as hers and put it back."

"Why didn't you just knock on her door and give it to her personally?" Roach asked.

I didn't have a good answer, so I went with a shrug.

If Roach had expected his little ambush to force a confession out of me, he didn't look very disappointed.

He changed tactics. "Fred Spencer is in a few of your classes, correct?"

I nodded.

"How well do you know him?"

Pretty darned well, I thought, and felt a blush begin in my cheeks, infuriated that I couldn't control it. "Not—not very. He's a bit out of my league."

Spivey bobbed his fool head up and down as if my comment needed his support. Roach seemed oblivious to his partner and continued with, "And Jessica Carter?"

For a moment I thought I was busted for sure. Someone must have seen me drop Jessica's water bottle in the trash, and they'd recovered it and found out about the niacin. How our little prank could possibly have anything to do with Penny's murder, I couldn't fathom. At a loss for excuses, I was on the verge of confessing all when I realized I didn't have to. I read Roach's mind and discovered the question was not designed to expose anything about me. Detective Roach was intensely curious about information that might implicate *Jessica.*

Interesting.

"I hardly know her," I said. "We've only had four days of school and Jessica's not exactly…well, she's popular."

Helpful Detective Spivey contributed another series of nods.

Roach said, "Rumor has it you and she had a little run-in."

"Not me." I didn't want to mention Gina in case he didn't know of her involvement.

He consulted his notepad again. I halfway expected him to drag Gina into it anyway, but instead, he stood. Spivey followed suit.

"Alright, Miss Strauss, Mrs. Strauss. We certainly appreciate your candor, and if you think of any information that might be at all relevant, please don't hesitate to contact me."

He handed Mom his card, and it looked to me like he held it a fraction too long before releasing it to her.

Once they'd gone, Mom turned to me. "Tainie!" Her voice dripped exasperation.

I wasn't sure which of Roach's revelations had set her off, so I trained my best puppy-dog eyes on her and waited.

She threw her hands into the air. "Why didn't you tell me this?"

"Which part?" I asked, trying not to sound sassy and aggravate her further.

She sighed and looked at me like I was a stranger. "Any of it. All of it. You never mentioned you'd had a run-in with a girl. And what was that malarkey about finding Penny's clothes in the laundry? You don't do the laundry—I do."

All would be disclosed to her as soon as Fred 'returned' her coat, so I took a deep breath and said, "I have a confession to make. Well, several confessions, but they all come together into one big…confession. Remember the storm..?"

Chapter Twenty-one

I had reached the part in my big reveal where I met with Fred this afternoon. As good as it felt to offload the tumult of emotions I'd been experiencing, there was one thing I wouldn't be discussing with my mother, no matter how understanding she'd been. I launched into an abbreviated and highly censored version of Tory's 'date,' but the telephone interrupted me.

The extension was sitting on the cluttered end table next to Gramma Foster's chair. She picked it up and said, "Hello?...Hello?" before hanging up.

Mom and I had been talking at the kitchen table in low voices. She got up and fetched a box of crackers, a knife and the almost empty jar of peanut butter. I began spreading it on a cracker as Mom said, "So now you're getting an idea of how difficult life can be in your condition."

"Geez, Mom, you make it sound like a disease or something. 'My condition.'"

She tilted her head Gramma's way. "She's hard of hearing and her memory is shot, but she's not stupid. The best way to protect those we love is by keeping this secret very, very close. You want me to call it–"

The phone rang again and Gramma snatched it up. "Yes?"

When she hung up this time she called, "No heavy breathing, just dead air. Must be some kid playing with the phone."

For no reason I could discern, I knew the phone calls were not an accident. When it rang again, Mom said, "Just let the machine get it, Edna."

We sat in silence as the answering machine my step-grandmother had had for at least a decade, the old-fashioned kind with an actual mini-cassette tape, began to play her message.

Gramma's voice sounded younger and quite breezy. "You've reached the residence of–"

"NO!" I shouted, lunging across the kitchen to get to the machine. I ripped the phone cord out of the wall, but not before Gramma's recorded voice said, "Edna Foster..."

I stood there with the cord dangling from my hand, staring at Mom, who stared back. She must have figured out why I'd done it, because instead of asking, she went for the extension and pushed a few buttons. "The last call says, 'Wireless Caller,' but there's no number."

Gramma lowered the footstool on her lounge chair with an abrupt clunk of the mechanism and, in the laborious bent-over waddle of a creaky old person who really shouldn't get up quickly, made her way into the kitchen. She glared from the frayed wire in my hand to the little plug still stuck in the wall.

"What's gotten into you?"

"I—I heard there was this—band of robbers who call and…"

"Nonsense!" Gramma snapped.

She opened the 'George drawer,' as she called it, a big, deep drawer that held anything and everything that didn't have a proper place. A moment of rummaging and she produced a new cord.

"Please exchange this for the one you ruined. And is that the last of the peanut butter?!"

I set to fixing the cord while Mom said, "Now Edna, you know peanut butter gets under your dentures."

"To hell with the dentures!" Gramma exclaimed. She grasped her top teeth and, with a disgusting sucking sound, forcibly removed them from her mouth. "I wan pea'nuh budda."

She took the knife and jar back to her chair and sat with a huff, leaving her glistening uppers in the middle of the table.

I said quietly, "Shouldn't she take her bottom teeth out, too?"

Before Mom could respond, Gramma practically shouted, "My boddom deeth are real. E'en someone in *your condition* shoulda figured thad oud."

Mom and I exchanged a look of alarm as Gramma cackled and put a hand to her ear. "thaaadth ride, I can hear e'erything you thay thankth to my truhthty Whithperthoft 2000."

I said quietly, "Oh, no! She hath a Whithperthoft 2000? Whatever will we do?"

Mom and I burst out laughing.

"Yuk it up, Ladieth," Gramma said. She waved the remote control at us in a mock-threatening gesture before cranking the volume on the television and effectively drowning us out.

It didn't take long for Mom and me to sober up. I wasn't as concerned about Gramma Foster overhearing us as I was about the phone calls.

"Am I just being paranoid?"

Mom shook her head. "After you left today, Seamus told me the Guild wasn't the only group you had to watch out for. They're fanatics who want to destroy the crown, or at least keep it out of the hands of the folk. Seamus said they haven't actually killed anyone—that he knows of, anyway— for centuries. Of course everyone's pretty much been in hiding that long, but do you remember the man in charge of the scientific ship we were on?"

I shook my head. "I was too busy barfing."

"Well, he and his crew obviously knew about the folk, and now I guess the British government is sniffing around."

"You think the British government is crank calling us?"

Mom puffed her cheeks out in frustration. "Tainie, this is not a joke. None of it."

"I know." I hesitated, thinking about the phone calls and that strange feeling I had that whoever was on the other end was up to no good. "Mom…I knew whoever was calling us was, I don't know, bad."

She smiled grimly. "Me, too. That's just plain old Irish intuition. Don't ever second-guess it."

In the morning, Mom was asleep on the couch. It was too hard on her body clock to switch back to daytime-living on her days off, so she usually stayed up all night watching television or reading. Sometimes she crocheted, a habit she picked up I think just to irritate Gramma Foster, who turned her nose up at it. I guess in knitting circles, crochet was some kind of red-headed step-child. The whole petty conflict made me vow never to take up either when I got old. Then I remembered I wasn't destined to get old and suddenly found myself weighing the benefits of crochet versus knitting.

I got ready as quietly as I could and snuck out of the house without waking Mom. Gramma's coat was still damp, so I wore Mom's windbreaker, which turned out to be completely inadequate. Two inches of snow covered the ground and more was falling. The air was sharp and cold in my lungs and by the time I got to school, my feet were frozen and I was shivering. I spent the last half of the walk thinking of ways a shapeshifter could make money for new clothes and the only thing I came up with was entering myself in a dog show.

Jessica must have fully recovered, because she was sitting in her seat in English. She wasn't glaring at Gina, a trend I hoped would continue. Fred glanced up at me and winked, which gave me a warm feeling. Like everyone else with working eyeballs, he thought I was ugly, but he always went out of his way to be nice. He and Tory had made plans to meet again today after school, and it would be a massive understatement to say I was looking forward to it.

Mr. Collins kept his lecture to an unprecedented five minutes and assigned us some reading. When the bell rang, Gina waited for me. Jessica was the one to rush out into the hallway. After Fred had gone past, I asked in a low voice, "Did she say anything to you this morning?"

Gina's expressive face registered shock and awe. "She came up to me and asked me to apologize for calling her a skeeze. Said she didn't know why everyone thought she was going to fight me, but she wasn't."

"Did you apologize?"

"Faster than the speed of light."

"Wow."

Gina and I parted ways for our respective classes at the main hallway intersection where the banner for the Bulldogs hung. Mr. Applebee was monitoring the hall again. I felt his eyes on me as I passed and wondered if he had anything to do with Jessica's magnanimous forgiveness.

I had quizzes in both Algebra and History, and in Art we had to get up and share our watercolors with the class. By the time lunch rolled around, my name was Titania "Stressed Out" Strauss.

The cafeteria was crowded again because of the snow, which had been gently falling this morning, but had become a howling blizzard. Even though it was Friday, the general atmosphere in the overly warm and humid space seemed subdued. I didn't know whether to attribute that to the weather, which couldn't decide if it wanted to be spring or winter or what, or to the announcement over the loudspeaker that a memorial 'service' would be held in the quad after school for Penny.

Tamika was back at the Loser table sitting with Gina, who had her notebook open and was tapping at the keys.

"Hey," I said, sitting across from them at the end of the table.

"Can't talk." The bottom half of Tamika's face was hidden behind a textbook. "Gotta study for a quiz in Algebra."

"Mrs. Lee?" I asked.

"Yeah."

"It's not that hard. Mostly multiple-choice."

She let the book fall to the table. "Thank the Lord."

I opened the lunch sack Mom had thoughtfully packed for me and realized it hadn't been that thoughtful after all. There was no way I was going to peel and eat two hardboiled eggs, as if everybody didn't already think the Loser table stunk. Instead, I nibbled on crackers and tried not to look too longingly at Tamika's peanut butter and jelly sandwich.

Gina appeared to be enthralled by whatever was on her notebook screen, so I looked around me while I ate. Fred and Jessica were at the same table, at opposite ends. He was sitting next to his blonde friend, whose name

I finally figured out by reading his jersey. 'Barkley' was chatting with a girl at the table behind him. Fred had a distant look on his face, a dreamy kind of smile playing around his mouth. I tried, but couldn't read him from here. It tickled me no end to imagine he was probably thinking of Tory.

"What are you so happy about?" Gina interrupted my reverie.

"N-nothing. Just—glad the whole Jessica thing is straightened out."

Gina made a 'humph' sound and turned her notebook around. "Read this."

It was an article in the local online newspaper about Penny. Most of it I already knew, like the part where the police confirmed they suspected homicide. There was a statement from Detective Roach, "If anyone has information regarding Penny Wharton's whereabouts in the early morning hours yesterday, please contact police." But the real surprise was a quote from Penny's mother. "A vicious coward took my baby from me and dumped her body like it was trash. She was an absolute angel; she did nothing to deserve this. I pray that God reveals whoever's responsible, and that they beg his forgiveness and come forward."

There was nothing new in either quote, but I'd been privy to the at-the-top-of-their-lungs conversations between Penny and her mother. Granted, Mrs. Wharton was grieving, but the names I'd heard her shriek at her daughter were far and away different from 'absolute angel,' not to mention the myriad and profane ways Mrs. Wharton had abused the God she now called upon.

Gina seemed to be waiting for me to respond, but I wasn't sure what I was supposed to infer from the article. She looked around and said, "Didn't you see the part about J?"

I assumed 'J' was code for Jessica.

I looked back at the screen, at a complete loss. Gina pulled the notebook around so we could both see it. "Right here. It says P worked at Ravenous. So does J, so they must know each other. And this morning, I overheard some girls saying that she and P hated each other."

That little tidbit must have been what sparked Detective Roach's interest in Jessica. Gina, who was already understandably inclined to believe the worst of Jessica, seemed to be convinced now that she had something to do with Penny's death. Or, as the police suspected, murder.

"What's Ravenous?" I asked.

Gina looked at me impatiently. "It's a clothing store at the mall. You and me, we don't shop there."

"Me neither," Tamika spoke up. "The largest size is like a six."

I thought about how Mrs. Z. was so eager to give back Mom's clothes after Penny died. "Maybe that's why 'J' wanted to bury the hatchet with you. She doesn't need anyone saying anything bad about her."

"That's what I thought!" Gina said, and then lowered her voice when several kids looked over. "I figure J killed P and now she's trying to allay suspicion by making nice with everyone."

"But why did she kill her?" Tamika asked. "Hating someone and killing them are two different animals."

Gina's face took on a calculating cast. "I have a theory, but it involves some speculation."

No kidding, I thought.

"Let's say P was seeing Stephen Spencer," Gina said.

"The golfer? She was?" This from Tamika, because I knew from Fred it was true.

"Yeah. Let's say. And we all know J has a thing for F."

"Who's 'F'? Fred?" Tamika looked around and I saw her eyes come to rest on the table where Fred and Jessica sat.

"Don't look!" Gina hissed.

"Sorry," Tamika muttered, looking down at her still-open Algebra book.

"Sheesh. Fred is Stephen's brother." Tamika made an 'oh' with her mouth. Gina pretended to read her notebook for a moment before continuing quietly, "So yesterday me and Tainie saw F get into his brother's car. P was also in the car."

"Really?" This was all news to Tamika, but I spoke up, "P was home after we saw her. I know because I heard her and her mom fighting at like two in the morning."

Gina bit her lip and shot me a look. "And you didn't feel this information was worth mentioning?"

I shrugged. "Didn't realize we were going to take a ride in the Mystery Machine."

Gina smiled. "I told you I loved this stuff."

She'd actually told me she wanted to be a pathologist, but I didn't argue the point.

"So why did J hate P?"

Gina leaned forward on her elbows. "J tried out for the cheerleading squad when she was a freshman, but P shot her down."

"That's it?" Tamika asked. "If I hated everyone who shot me down…"

"I know, right?" Gina grinned. "I don't get that whole cheerleader personality. You gotta be real obsessive to maintain that happy-happy joy-joy vibe all day long. Anyway, I'm stopping by P's thing this afternoon to see if J is there showing the proper amount of grief. You guys wanna come?"

"I have to babysit," Tamika said.

I have a date, I thought with a secret rush of pleasure, but said, "Can't."

Gina shrugged. "Okay, but you're gonna miss out on the spectacle."

My eyes slid to where Fred sat. I wasn't going to miss out on anything.

Chapter Twenty-two

It was Friday of the first week of school, and Chemistry was the last class of the day. We had a quiz; I hadn't lied to Mom about that, but I hadn't studied at all. As the answers to question after question eluded me, I imagined I felt for the first time in my life like a normal teen. I was always prepared. I always studied. But here I was, struggling to answer what I suspected were pretty simple questions, and the only excuse I had was sitting next to me, tapping his pencil on his closed textbook.

The wall of windows looking out on the courtyard showed drifts of snow piling up everywhere. The statue of Ambrose P. Ashworth was cloaked in white, like he had a fluffy shawl draped over his shoulders.

Mr. Applebee stood at the front of the class, hand resting on the counter between Jessica and Gina, eyes roaming over the students. His gaze swung my way and he briefly caught my eye. I don't know why I did it, but I tried to read him. It was strange, but I didn't get anything other than a strong impression of avoidance. But he'd turned away so quickly, I doubt I read him properly.

Fred finished his quiz first and got up to place it on Mr. Applebee's desk. Gina was second. I checked off random answers for the questions I didn't know and deposited my sheet on top of Gina's, feeling like a fraud.

Jessica was hunched over her paper when I went by. I hadn't seen her glare at Gina once.

The wind rattled the windows with a whistling moan and the lights flickered briefly and went out. Normally, daylight coming in from outside would make the fluorescent overhead lights obsolete, but the storm had artificially darkened the sky. Without the lights, the chemistry lab was a gloomy, foreign place.

A murmur rose from the class and Mr. Applebee said, "Hold on a sec," and went to rummage in a cupboard. He turned and began tossing things to the students. Fred caught one—it was a glow stick. Bright green lights popped up all over the room.

"Chemiluminescence," Mr. Applebee said loudly. "Extra credit for whoever can tell me what that means."

Given the dismal grade I was sure to get on the quiz, I decided to go for it for once and raised my hand.

"Miss Strauss!" Mr. Applebee boomed.

"It's a chemical reaction that emits light and heat."

"Very good! Anyone know what two chemicals make glow sticks glow?"

Fred's hand was the only one to join mine in the air.

"Mr. Spencer!"

"Hydrogen peroxide and phenol oxylate ester," Fred said.

I looked at him adoringly.

"And how did you come by that information?" Mr. Applebee asked.

"Halloween 2006. My mom called the poison control center after my big brother dared me to drink one," Fred replied.

Everyone except Mr. Applebee laughed. "Alright class, simmer down. Those of you who have not completed your quizzes now have adequate light to do so."

The lights stayed off for the rest of class. I tried to focus on the lesson after the quiz was over, because I didn't want to take another disastrous test, but the mounds of snow outside distracted me. Was Fred still planning on meeting me in the woods after school? I wished I could ask him.

Gina waited for me after class. Due to the 'inclement weather,' Penny's memorial had been cancelled, so Gina and I began the slow, cold trudge home. There weren't a lot of drivers on the road, and those that did attempt the weather crept slowly past on the slick streets, with the exception of the driver of a blue Mustang convertible with the top up. We heard his pounding bass from a block away, but it quickly gained volume as the Mustang fishtailed its way up the street, engine revving.

"That's Fred's brother!" Gina said as the car sped past. We witnessed it as Stephen Spencer lost control, spinning out in a full circle, sheets of wet snow spraying everywhere. It seemed for a moment like he was going to regain control, but instead the car shot off at an angle and plowed through a row of hedges before coming to rest facing backwards in the middle of someone's front yard.

When Stephen opened the door, wedging it into a show bank, the music got much louder. I'd heard the song before but didn't know what it was called. He stood on the running board, bracing himself on the door with one hand. With the other hand he gesticulated grandly in time with the beat as he sang along with the female lead, "I can feel you all around me, thickening the air I'm breathing!"

Gina and I were frozen in place across the street from the spectacle, two blocks from Ashworth. There were other knots of kids hanging around, too. It was a miracle Stephen hadn't hit anyone. After less than a minute watching him humiliate himself, we saw Fred run up. He slipped and fell twice before he made it to his brother's car and then he shoved at Stephen until he got him back into the car. The music stopped. From where we stood, I could hear their voices, but not what was said. Fred sounded angry and Stephen's laughter echoed out of the vehicle despite the dampening effect of the snow.

"Dang," Gina said quietly.

"Let's go." I grabbed her arm, but she shook me off.

"I want to see what happens."

Fred's friend Barkley had come up to him and he and Fred waded through the snow to get behind the car. They appeared to be trying to push it back into the street.

"They need help," I said.

Gina held her hands up as if to say, "What can we do?"

It was too late anyway. Flashing lights heralded the arrival of a police cruiser. I saw Fred throw his arms up in defeat. Maybe it was the strength of his emotions, but even though he was across the street and down some, I was certain I could read him. Stephen was about to be arrested for drunk driving.

"I can't watch this," I muttered, turning towards home. Gina caught up to me several yards away.

"What's your deal?" she asked. "You don't…*like* Fred, do you? Because I hate to break it to ya, but he's…"

"So far out of my league we might as well be different species? I'm aware of that."

And as far as I knew, we *were* different species.

As we walked, Gina took off her glasses and wiped the accumulated snowdrops on the underside of her coat sleeve. It was the first time I'd seen her without them. Under her hazel eyes, which were much larger than they appeared from behind the thick lenses, dark circles told me she'd probably worn glasses since she was a child.

"You know why they call it a crush?" she asked finally.

"I don't have a crush on him! He's nice to me, that's all."

"Okay." She didn't sound convinced. "I gotta get home and thaw out. Have a nice weekend."

"Every weekend is a nice weekend." I don't know why I said it; it was one of my mom's favorite quotes even though she hadn't had a genuine ‘weekend’ in years.

Gina chuckled and waved as she split off toward her house. I looked back down the street, trying to catch one last glimpse of Fred, but couldn’t see anything past tree trunks and parked cars covered in snow.

My fingers, toes, ears and face were almost numb from cold by the time I walked into Gramma’s condo.

Mom was still asleep on the couch and Gramma must have been napping in her room. I snuck into the bedroom. At first, I thought Mom must have gotten up to do some laundry, but the folded piles of clothing on the bed didn’t look familiar. There were jeans and shirts, two jackets, and lined up on the floor alongside the mattress were two pairs of shoes and some snow boots, size 10.

“They’re used.”

I turned to find Mom standing in the doorway.

“Wow, where did you–” I stopped, and my dismay must have been all over my face because Mom said quickly, “They weren’t Penny’s! I took the bus to Salvation Army before the snow got bad.”

She held one of the shirts up against me. “See, it’s kinda cute and you can wear it when you’re…Tory.”

Right then I finally understood what it meant to feel your heart in your throat. I threw my arms around her. Face pressed against her chest, I choked out, “You’re the best Mom in the whole world, you know that?”

She hugged me back tightly. “That’s been my goal, lo these seventeen years.”

We laughed. The moment didn’t have a chance to get awkward because the phone rang. Mom pulled away, brushed the hair out of my eyes and left me to gleefully paw through my ‘new to me’ wardrobe.

In a few minutes she was back, looking pale and upset.

“What’s wrong?”

She closed her eyes and put a hand to her forehead. For a moment I thought she wasn’t going to tell me.

Then she said flatly, “Seamus is missing.”

Chapter Twenty-three

Mom summed up the phone call for me. Apparently, the woman on the line had an English accent and told Mom she was Seamus' partner, a word I knew to be the English version of 'significant other.' She claimed to have been at the airport waiting to pick him up, but he never showed. She begged Mom to call Caitlin. Mom told her she had no idea how to get hold of Caitlin, which was true. Before hanging up, the woman said, "If that's the case, then Seamus is done for."

"She actually said, 'done for?'" I asked.

"Those very words."

"Weird. Is it just me, or did that sound like a threat?"

"I thought so. Remember the calls we got last night?"

I nodded.

"Well, the way I contacted Seamus a few days ago was to send an email to the same address he had up on his website during the Cataclysm. I wasn't sure it would still work, but then he called. His call said 'Wireless Caller' with no number, just like last night."

"You think someone kidnapped him and then called all the numbers on his phone?"

Mom made a 'bingo!' face at me.

I said, "If she really was his 'partner,' would she know where to find Caitlin?"

"You heard him—he doesn't trust anyone. If she really was his partner, she wouldn't even know about Caitlin. And she wouldn't have known how to find us."

I held up a finger. "He either told her," I held up another finger, "or she has access to his computer, or hacked into it and got our number from the email you sent," another finger, "or the bad guys have his phone and she's one of them."

"The important thing is, we can't believe what anyone tells us; especially not people who call and ask us to find Caitlin for them."

I thought about Seamus' missing arm. He hadn't come right out and said that he'd lost it to torture, but I inferred it anyway.

"What did you say in the email?"

"Nothing that would give you away. But I think you should stop shifting. At least until we're sure you're not being watched."

I thought about Fred waiting in the frozen woods for Tory. He'd be depressed about his brother, worried about his mother. If Tory didn't show, he'd be devastated. Would I really be risking my life if I ignored Mom's advice and decided to meet him?

If I changed into Tory from the condo and walked out all bundled up for the weather, no one could possibly be the wiser. I would have to wait until after Mom left for work, and she would probably see Fred waiting for me, but I was willing to bet she wouldn't say anything to him. She had no official connection to Tory.

"You're probably right," I said, trying to inject the right note of disappointment into my voice. "But what about Seamus? That woman is either his partner or his kidnapper. Either way, we have to assume he's in trouble. Do we just…ignore it?"

Mom frowned. "Yes. We have to ignore it. We can't call the police. What would we tell them? And even if I knew where to find Caitlin, this could be some kind of ruse to lure her out of hiding."

I knew she was right. "This sucks."

She pulled me into another hug. "There's no way to say this nicely: it's your new reality, sweetie. If we lie low and don't give them a reason to suspect you're a shapeshifter, maybe they'll leave us alone."

Later, I was in luck. It was Gramma Foster's bridge night and soon after she woke from her nap, she spiffed herself up in preparation to going to Mrs. Zimmerman's house.

When I questioned it, she scoffed and said, "So she took Sophie's clothes. She gave them back, what's the big deal? Sometimes people do strange things. You just wait until you get old—you'll see how much fun it is."

The comment resurrected that conflicted feeling I got whenever I thought of not getting old; gratitude that my mind and body would not fail me and sadness that my life would not follow the normal course of birth, life, death.

Gramma and Mom left at the same time, so I didn't have to invent another excuse for when I took off. I gave Mom a fifteen minute head start and then I dressed in one of my new 'Tory' outfits and shapeshifted.

The warmest of my two new jackets was black with a fake-fur lined hood, and when I left the condo, the hood was up and cinched tightly around my face. I'd borrowed some of Mom's lipstick; just a smidge of a neutral pink so Tory wouldn't look too pale. I was hoping that by the time I got home it would be gone—all kissed away.

The snow had stopped. All told, it looked like we'd gotten around a foot, but it was hard to be sure with the wind blowing it around.

Inside the new snow boots, my feet slid from toe to heel and back again with every step. They fit me well, but were too big for Tory. I scanned the area as I left the complex and headed toward the park. It was silent. No one was out in the cold, not even kids making snowmen. No faces peered out of windows at me; no shady characters sat in their car spying. On the sidewalk, a lone set of tracks in the snow, almost obliterated by the wind, showed my mother's path before me.

The woods seemed less spooky under the blanket of white. The fresh scent of wood smoke and pine floated on the air, and everything glistened in the fading light. Someone was sitting on Fred's rock, but as I neared, I realized it wasn't him. I ducked behind the same tree as before, thinking my Mom had faked me out and was about to bust me. But someone else's voice rang out in a mocking sing-song.

"I saw you!"

To my astonishment the voice belonged to Jessica.

Before I even had time to ask myself why she could possibly be here, she called, "Fred asked me to wait for you. He won't be meeting you anymore!"

She was coming closer; I heard the *whup whup* of her footsteps as she made her way across the creek, and then the crunch of her boots on the path. I pressed my back against the tree, unsure of whether I was more scared or angry, but there was no way I was going to let her get the upper hand. She was only seconds away from finding me cowering like a mouse when I straightened up, untied my hood and pushed it back. Then I shifted and stepped out.

She gasped and stopped in her tracks, a look of abject horror forming on her face.

"Hello Jessica." I spoke coldly.

Her shaking hand came up seemingly of its own accord, finger pointing accusingly. "You—you're…"

"Dead? Yes."

She stumbled backward, tripped, and fell on her backside in the snow. A tremulous scream erupted from her mouth, too weak for anyone to hear.

"Stop that," I said.

She stopped, staring up at me, face white as the ghost she supposed I must be.

"Why did you kill me, Jessica?"

Her face twisted into an awful grimace. "I didn't, Penny! I swear to God I didn't have anything to do with it!"

I read her mind and she was telling the truth. I sighed. Now what?

But she wasn't finished. "Didn't you see him? Your killer?"

"No, I didn't see him," I said impatiently. "He hit me from behind. Would I be accusing you if I knew who did it?"

"N–no, of course not." Jessica's shrill laugh sounded hysterical.

"Go home!" I said, trying to inject a ghoulish thunder in my voice.

She scrambled to her feet. "Okay. No problem."

But she didn't leave.

"Penny…I…I'm sorry about what happened. I'm sorry we weren't friends. What's it like being dead? Did you go to heaven?"

Oh, my gosh, she did not just ask me that. Think fast.

"No, I didn't go to heaven. Not yet—you know how it works. I have to solve my murder first, and then I get to go into the light. But while I'm here, I'm going to give you some advice: stop chasing Fred. He's not interested in you, and the girl you were waiting for wouldn't fall for your lie. She's not stupid."

Jessica's mouth fell open and stayed that way as she clearly struggled to find a suitable response. I probed her mind and discovered how she knew Fred was meeting me: Fred told Barkley who told one of her friends, who told her. She'd come to spy on Tory and Fred—but Fred had been and gone. I experienced a flash of sorrow at missing him, but to my dismay, Jessica began to cry. "But I love him!"

"Oh, you do not! In order to love someone, you have to know them. What you have is a crush. You know why they call it that?"

She nodded miserably.

I needed to wrap this little freak show up. The longer I talked with her, the more comfortable she got in my presence. The last thing I wanted was for her to get all chummy with my Penny specter. I was not about to go into the guidance-from-beyond-the-grave business. I sent a silent apology to the real Penny and said, "I want you to go home and take a hard look at your life. You don't want to make bad decisions like I did and end up at the bottom of a pool."

She was still crying, but she nodded. To my relief, she went past me and began to walk towards the park. But before she got more than ten feet, she stopped.

"Penny?"

"Yeah?"

"I think Mr. Applebee knows something."

"What?"

She looked over her shoulder. "I saw him a couple of times this week in the food court. He was watching you, I'm pretty sure."

I had never been to the local mall, but maybe the food court was situated near Ravenous, the store where Jessica and Penny worked.

"Did you tell the police?"

She shook her head. "He gives me the creeps, but I never saw him do anything. I didn't want to get him in trouble for nothing. It's a feeling I have, that's all."

I looked at her tear-stained face, suddenly feeling sorry for her. "Trust your intuition. But find another boy to like, okay?"

She didn't agree with me, but her face crumpled, like she'd already accepted the necessity and it really hurt. After she'd gone, I had a choice between following her or going the opposite direction towards Fred's house. I chose to avoid the park. If I turned right as soon as I exited the line of trees separating the woods from Fred's grandparent's land, I'd only be a few dozen yards from the public sidewalk. Then I could skirt around the block and get to my complex from the other side. It would add significant time to the journey, but it wasn't like I had plans anymore.

I hopped carefully across the icy creek boulders, and when I came out from the trees, I looked longingly towards Fred's house. There was no one to be seen and no tracks marring the wide expanse of snow blanketing the property. No smoke rose from the huge stone chimney. The snowfall along the tree line was thin, so the walk was easier than I'd expected. I came out to the sidewalk, which someone, probably the Spencer's gardener, had already shoveled.

I hurried along, torn between wondering why Fred hadn't waited very long and thinking about what Jessica had said.

Stephen would be in jail, his family scrambling to get him released. Fred's time had probably been limited; it was likely he'd only waited in order to tell me he couldn't stay.

Jessica's revelation about Mr. Applebee was irrelevant to me. I would not be passing it along to the police—how could I? It's not like I could tell anyone how I'd come by the knowledge. Jessica would either tell them what she suspected or she wouldn't. Still, I couldn't see Mr. Applebee, gentle giant that he was, attacking and killing an innocent girl.

I reached the end of the shoveled sidewalk and had to plod through the snow in my oversized boots. Just as I realized I should change back into myself so the boots would fit—that in fact, I was still walking around as Penny—a car that I'd idly assumed had been slowly navigating the slick road came to a halt in the middle of the street.

I looked into the vehicle, couldn't see the passenger, but the driver was a short-haired woman, and she was staring right at me with an outraged look on her face.

Oh, no!

Whoever the woman was, she clearly recognized Penny, a girl who was supposed to be dead.

I did an abrupt about-face, threw my arms up to cover my head, and shifted. To make the boots fit in case I needed to run, I chose to become myself rather than Tory. I walked quickly back the way I had come, listening as a car door slammed. I tried to act cool, kept to the sidewalk, kept walking, but I heard footsteps come up behind me.

After convincing Mom I wasn't going to shift and after the encounter with Jessica in the woods, I was becoming more confident in my ability to tell a lie. Whoever was about to accost me would see that they'd been mistaken. It was not Penny's doppelganger they had seen, but a girl who looked nothing like the murdered young woman. I would do nothing to try to help this person understand what they thought they'd seen. I would give them a strange look and walk on.

I'd just gotten past the line of trees and glimpsed Fred's house when a heavy hand came down on my shoulder. It was the passenger who spun me around—I know, because the car pulled up at the curb next to me just before he did it.

"Mr. Collins!" I cried, genuinely confused. His eyes were narrowed into furious slits and his teeth were bared like he was handling rotten meat.

"You!" he exclaimed. "How many of you are there?"

The question sent a shaft of dreadfully cold fear through my gut.

"What do you m–?"

"Don't deny it!" He shook me so hard I felt like a rag doll. I hadn't been aware of the driver getting out and opening the back door of the car, but Mr. Collins suddenly shoved me towards it. I only got my wits about me at the last second; barely in enough time to grab the edge of the doorframe to stop my forward momentum for a moment. Before I could kick, fight, scream, he put his shoulder to my back and forced me inside.

Chapter Twenty-four

If Mr. Collins had a gun, I never saw it. He did nothing to keep me quiet other than give me a threatening look that sealed my jaw shut like superglue. The driver, a forty-something woman with broad shoulders and a thickish neck, drove silently. The fact that they didn't prevent me from seeing where we were going scared me more than anything. I watched movies; if they planned to release me from wherever they were taking me, surely I'd be wearing a fashionable blindfold.

We didn't go far and our destination wasn't the abandoned warehouse I expected. The woman reached up and pressed a button on a gadget fastened to the visor. A white garage door slowly opened on a nondescript tan house in an older development. Even with my unobstructed view of the neighborhood, I had no idea where we were. I had never gone farther in this town than the grocery store less than a mile from Gramma Foster's condo. I had never been to the museums, to downtown, or to any of the movie theatres in our corner of suburban Philadelphia.

I knew before I saw him that Seamus would be in the house. What surprised me beyond words, had I been brave enough to utter any, was that he sat in relative comfort on a bed in one of the back rooms. The windows had been shuttered, but Seamus was not chained to a brick wall as I had feared. He immediately sent me a message when I was patted down and shoved into the room.

I don't think they're Guild. They don't seem to know about iron.

That didn't mean they wouldn't and couldn't kill us or that we were in any way safe from harm, but I was relieved nonetheless.

Mr. Collins shut the door behind me and I heard the unmistakable click of not one, but several bolts locking. Seamus smiled grimly and spoke again in my mind. *We are being monitored.*

Out loud, he said, "Titania. Did they hurt you?"

"No. What's going on? What do they want from us?" I thought it best to play completely dumb for the cameras that pointed down at us from all four corners of the room.

Good, Seamus sent. "They haven't told me much, just asked a lot of questions that don't make sense." *They appear to be working for the British government.*

In order to seem innocent to our watchers, I knew I'd have to bombard Seamus with questions myself, so I did. I asked all the obvious who, what, where questions I could think of, and he answered most of them with, "I don't know."

"Are they kidnapping us? Mom doesn't have any money to pay ransom." It wasn't hard to produce some authentic tears. I sniffed pathetically and sat next to him on the bed.

"Don't cry. This is some kind of terrible mistake. We'll be okay."

He put his arm, the one that shouldn't be there, around my shoulders and patted me gently. I sent, *Are they going after Mom, too*?

He replied, *If they are rounding the folk up, count on it.*

How are we going to get out of here?

It was what I didn't want to hear: the same answer he'd given me for all my out-loud questions, *I don't know.*

Without appearing to be doing more than looking around despondently, I took a thorough inventory of the contents of the room. It was a back bedroom in a small house, maybe ten feet square. The carpet was a worn, stained beige that had impressions where two heavy items of furniture had formerly rested against the far wall. The doors had been removed from the closet, as well as the hanger bar. The locked interior door was probably hollow particleboard and the hinges were mounted on the other side. The wooden hurricane shutters over the one small window had been installed on the inside and appeared to have been screwed shut. Light filled the room from a bare bulb in the middle of the low ceiling that had some kind of cage around it instead of a glass fixture. The bed was a mattress, sans box spring, resting on a solid black base. There was one pillow and a faded blue bedspread. Seamus had either not slept here, or he'd smoothed the cover into place when he awoke.

It seemed to me that the four cameras were overkill, but I guessed the purpose was to keep us under surveillance at all times. If we somehow took out a camera each, our watchers would have time to get to us before we could get to the other two. Assuming the watchers were in the house with us, which I did.

I looked at Seamus. *How many are there*?

I've only seen the man and woman who brought you, but I heard another man's voice last night.

I had no idea how long I'd been there, probably less than an hour, when the door opened. I halfway expected Seamus to do something, but he sat calmly. The woman stepped partially in and set a white paper bag and two drinks in disposable cups with straws on the floor. She left without saying a word.

Seamus muttered, "Finally. I'm starved," and retrieved the food. He had a burger hanging out of his mouth before he even sat back down. He offered me the other burger, but I declined.

I did take one of the sodas, though. It had been a long time since I'd experienced the bubbly goodness of a bona fide cola. The refreshing coolness burned my throat in a pleasant, familiar way.

"What do we do if we have to use the restroom?" I asked.

He shrugged, cheeks bulging with burger. I'd never seen anyone eat so much so quickly.

"Haven't you gone?"

He frowned and shook his head.

I had second thoughts about drinking the soda. In this tiny room, there literally wasn't a pot to pee in. On the other hand, maybe if my bladder created an urgent situation, our captors would reveal more of the house when they escorted me to the bathroom.

I'd gulped down about half my soda by the time Seamus took his first sip.

"Does this taste funny to you?" he asked.

It had. At first I thought it was diet, but none of the buttons on the plastic lid were depressed. Then I attributed it to a mix up in the carbonation/syrup ratio, a not unheard-of thing in fast food joints. I still relished every drop, even with the funky after-taste.

I looked at Seamus, about to question why he asked, but the motion of turning my head set it to spinning. I must have looked as dizzy as I felt because he snatched the drink out of my hand and hurled it against the door. Soda splattered everywhere. I felt drops of it hit my face, but couldn't be bothered, all of a sudden, to wipe them off.

What happened next was somewhat of a blur. The door opened and Mr. Collins barged in—pointing a gun—but he didn't seem to be holding it very confidently. The thick-necked woman followed behind more hesitantly, balancing a silver tray with what looked like medical instruments on it.

Lost in a hazy horror of the possibilities the stack of hypodermic needles had in store for me, I was only vaguely aware of Seamus removing his shirt and unbuttoning his jeans until Mr. Collins aimed the gun at him and said, "Stop what you're doing."

Seamus, who was staring into Mr. Collins' face and must know whether the threat was real, ignored him and stepped out of his pants. I averted my gaze, and caught thick-neck's eye. Idly, I read her mind as she assessed my state of drugged-ness and dismissed me as a threat. Her goal was to get a sample of our blood for testing.

Well, finally, something that made sense.

I was still reading her mind when she looked at Seamus, and I giggled a little at her reaction to his nakedness. In her eyes, he was an attractive man with a lean, fit body. Did she know he was two thousand years old? That he was discarding his clothing in preparation to shift was obvious to me, but the woman thought whatever drug they'd given us had simply had a strange effect on him.

I giggled again. Silly lady. Seamus had only taken a sip. Despite the four cameras, they must not be watching us very closely. That thought set off little alarm bells in the back of my mind, but I was in no condition to figure out why.

Mr. Collins held the gun on Seamus, but seemed to think he needed reinforcements against a naked, unarmed man, because he called out, "Higgins!"

I snorted with laughter. Oh, no! A baddie named Higgins was on the way!

"Higgins!" I mimicked Mr. Collins, who gave me the barest glance of distaste. "Here higgie-higgie-higgie."

Seamus sent, *Fight it off. We metabolize drugs very quickly.*

I managed to sober myself up somewhat after that; at least I got the giggling under control, but I was still significantly giddy and my body felt heavy. The bed suddenly looked very inviting, so I flopped onto my back and watched the players in the room with a foggy lack of concern bordering on disinterest.

A young man wearing a Simpsons t-shirt appeared in the doorway. Chubby, with long hair and glasses, he seemed less like a 'Higgins' than a British agent, but it was close.

Mr. Collins glanced over at Higgins and began to say something, but quite unexpectedly, the gun flew out of his hand and hit the far wall. He grabbed his arm, which had sprouted three long bloody gashes.

Thick-neck screamed and dropped the tray of instruments with a metallic clang that reverberated in my head. I expected Higgins to produce a gun and begin shooting, but he turned and high-tailed it down the hall.

As grizzly bears go, Seamus made a smallish one, but reared up on his hind legs, he towered over Mr. Collins. And when he bared a mouthful of carnivorous teeth and let out a guttural roar, complete with a fine spray of spittle right in Mr. Collins' face, that brave man tried to hide behind the thick-necked nurse. It had been a near-instantaneous shift, taking even me by complete surprise.

I rolled to a slumped but upright position and then dropped to all fours on the carpet. My arms felt like noodles, but with as much speed as I could muster, I crawled across the floor and retrieved the gun. As soon as I picked it up, Seamus shifted back. Mr. Collins and the nurse cowered in the corner while Seamus dressed quickly. Then he took the gun from me, shoved the last bite of the second hamburger in his mouth and said, “Let’s go.”

I got unsteadily to my feet, wondering in a vague sort of way at how easy it had been to subdue Mr. Collins. If he was heading some kind of illegal British black ops team, they were more Get Smart than 007.

I looked at him holding his injured arm and watching us with narrowed eyes as we prepared to leave.

Wait a minute. Was that a smile on his face? A quick scan of his mind confirmed it. Underneath the significant pain he was feeling, I discovered we had done exactly what he wanted us to do. And it was all on tape.

Chapter Twenty-five

Seamus shut the bedroom door and threw the bolts, then headed down the hall in the direction Higgins had gone. The third door he tried was locked, so he knocked politely.

From inside, Higgins said, "Go away! I won't try to stop you if you just leave."

I leaned against the wall, feeling better, but still a little woozy.

Seamus said, "I'm a split second away from breaking this door down. Open it."

To my surprise, the door opened a crack. Seamus cautiously pushed his way in, gun at the ready.

It was a very small room; more like a walk-in closet. Higgins was standing next to an array of monitors and equipment. He raised both hands, palms out. "Dude, I didn't sign on for this. I'm just the tech guy!"

"Can they get out?" Seamus asked, nodding his head to one of the monitors that showed nurse Ratchet tending to Mr. Collins' injuries.

"Not if you locked the door."

Seamus glanced around the room. "Where's my bag?"

Higgins kept his hands in the air.

"Over there. They went through it pretty thoroughly and I wouldn't be surprised if they bugged it and put a tracking device somewhere in case you escaped."

I took a closer look at Higgins the Tech Guy. Unlike Mr. Collins, he was an American and seemed sincere in his lack of loyalty to my British 'teacher' and his ilk.

Seamus rummaged inside his bag. The only thing he removed was a single key.

"I gotta say," Higgins gushed, "you are one hella cool dude! I've never seen anything like what you did in there outside of the movies. I thought these guys were paranoid, but man! I'm on your side now, I swear. Read my mind, you'll see."

So they knew we could read minds, too. Who were these people?

Seamus only let out a short laugh as he pocketed the key. "I believe you."

"It's just—listen—don't let this lame house throw you off. These guys got some serious gear hidden in the rafters. Those cameras in there? Infrared, night vision, you name it. Plus the mattress was tracking your heart rate and respiration. They got that room hooked up with every kind of monitor known to man—even a Geiger counter!"

I asked, "What was that nurse going to do with our blood?"

Higgins shrugged. "Test it, I guess. Hey, they didn't tell us why they were doing all this."

"But now you know," Seamus said. His voice had dropped threateningly and I found myself praying he wasn't planning to eliminate all the witnesses.

Higgins must have had the same thought, because he said, "Dude, the cameras are all linked up to satellite. Every bit of information they gathered has already gone to whoever Collins works for."

Seamus said, "Where are the keys?"

"For the—oh, sure! No problem, I got you covered. Right this way."

Higgins kept his hands in the air all the way to the kitchen where a set of car keys sat on the counter next to a woman's purse.

"Is that the garage door?" Seamus asked. When Higgins said yes, Seamus gestured to it with his free hand. "After you."

The three of us left in the same car I'd been kidnapped in, me in the back seat and Higgins up front where Seamus could keep an eye on him. The friendly tech guy fell into what I suspected was an uncharacteristic silence as we drove. He was probably worried about his fate, but it turned out he needn't be. Seamus dropped him off several miles from the house.

Standing forlornly in his t-shirt in the freezing cold in an isolated warehouse district, Higgins waved and said, "Thanks for not killing me, guys."

Seamus depressed the button to roll up the window, but I said, "Wait!"

Higgins raised his eyebrows at me, looking hopeful, probably thinking I was going to plead his case to Seamus to let him back in the car so we could drop him off somewhere humane.

"How did they find us?" I asked.

His head went back and then he shook it. "Yeah, that I don't know. Sorry."

Seamus thanked him and said, "You've been kind, so I offer you a piece of intelligence you aren't likely to hear from your employers. Your knowledge of my abilities is highly privileged, however 'cool' you consider it to be. Your safety may very well rely upon your discretion."

"I signed a nondisclosure agreement, dude. Not that anyone would believe me if I opened my yap. Besides, Collins isn't the violent type, I can tell."

"He may be weak, but I have dealt with his kind before. They do the bidding of those in power, and you do not know what he may be capable of."

Higgins stepped back and shoved his hands in the pockets of his baggy jeans. It was getting dark and his breath came out in white puffs.

"Thanks for the warning. For what it's worth, I think you got a bum rap. They should be signing you up as a superhero instead of treating you like a freak."

Seamus laughed. "I have no desire to fight crime. Now if you'd be so kind as to hand me that mobile phone in your pocket, we'll be on our way."

Higgins didn't even try to hide the fact that he'd been caught. With undisguised reluctance, he handed his phone over. I could see it was the newest generation Internet slash multimedia whiz-bang gadget.

Higgins said, "I just bought that two weeks ago with the pay from this gig. I wasn't going to use it to send anyone after you; I just need to call a cab. It's cold out, and this is the middle of nowhere."

"There is a 7-11 two blocks north and three blocks east. I suggest you walk quickly to keep warm." Seamus drove away then, and I actually felt sorry for Higgins. On the plus side, I was beginning to feel normal as the effects of whatever they'd drugged me with wore off. After several minutes, I asked, "Where are we going?"

"There."

We were on a wide boulevard with increased traffic and stoplights at every corner. Seamus pointed to a strip mall with the requisite coffee shop, deli and dry cleaner. He parked in front of one of those postal stores that also offered copies and post office boxes. Inside, he used the key he'd retrieved from his bag to open a small box and withdraw a package.

"I got into the habit of creating documentation for alternate identities and stashing it and some emergency cash whenever I travel," he said. "You would be wise to adopt the practice."

Travel? Me? I'd never even considered it.

Instead of getting back into the car, Seamus began to stride across the parking lot and I trotted along next to him. We reached the sidewalk, which hadn't been shoveled, but there'd been enough foot traffic before us to reveal a narrow strip of wet sidewalk that was beginning to turn to ice.

When we got to a dark stretch between street lights, he bent down to retie his shoe. I didn't recognize him when he stood.

"You'd best disguise yourself," he said.

I nodded and flipped the hat on my new jacket up over my hair. Then I turned away from the lights of a passing car, bent and pretended to brush something off my lower leg. Once the imaginary lint had been taken care of, I straightened up—as Tory.

It was a Saturday night, and this particular street had either been plowed or had seen enough traffic to keep it free from snow. It was busy with people in their vehicles going about their business. Up ahead I saw a large lighted marquee sign that read, "Eastfield Mall."

"Buy a new outfit. Wait for me in the food court and then we'll go get your mom," Seamus said. He handed me a wad of bills and split off at the corner for a seedy-looking car rental place.

Inside the mall, fully half of the storefronts were gated and locked. The theater was humming, though, since a new animated film had been released—not the first film since the Cataclysm, but the first that was expected to become a blockbuster. The smell of hotdogs set my stomach to rumbling, but I wanted to follow Seamus' orders to the letter.

I counted the money he'd given me, astonished to find I held two hundred dollars in twenties in my suddenly sweaty hands. I hadn't had that much money since…well, ever.

I found my way to J.C. Penny and within minutes had an armful of clothes to try on. None of them fit, because I had no idea what size to get for Tory. A salesperson would be nice, but they were scarcer than a post-Cataclysm filet mignon. I chose my favorite of the jeans and tops and picked three sizes, finally getting it right.

It wasn't until I was walking past a clothes store on my way to the food court that I realized I should have changed into my new clothes. The trendy store had loud music blaring out into the mall, and someone must have recently spritzed an entire bottle of a noxious perfume into the air because the thick scent wafted over me as I passed. I glanced into the racks of skimpy-despite-the-fact-that-it-wasn't-quite-spring clothes and there was Jessica, staring my way. Sure enough, the sign above the store-front said 'Ravenous' in a funky neon font. I'd forgotten Gina said Jessica worked there.

She was looking past a dark-haired guy with his back to me—but I'd seen Fred from the back enough times to recognize him.

I panicked for a moment until I realized Jessica had never met Tory. If I kept walking, I'd be fine. I willed my heartbeat to calm down, averted my face and took one step after another towards the safety of the tables in the large, but nearly empty, food court. Just when I thought I was home free, I felt a hand on my arm.

It was Jessica of course. She spun me around and I saw that Fred hadn't followed her. He also hadn't, from the look on his face, realized that the girl she'd abandoned their conversation to catch up with was me—Tory. He started towards us.

"Where did you get that jacket?" Jessica demanded.

I glanced down at it, feigning surprise. "I don't know. It's old. Why?"

"Because I saw it on someone else today."

"Not this jacket," I said.

Fred had arrived and was staring at me uncomprehendingly. I didn't need to read his mind to know he was wondering how I knew Jessica.

"Yes that jacket!" Her voice had risen dramatically. I understood where she was coming from: she'd seen a ghost today and that ghost had been dressed exactly like me. Was I surprised she hadn't taken Penny's advice to stay away from Fred? No, but technically, Fred seemed to have sought her out.

Despite a flash of jealousy, I smiled at him, said, "Hey," and brushed past her.

"What are you doing here?" he asked.

"You know her?" Jessica's voice had reached shriek proportions.

I gave her my best 'are you insane?' look and asked, "Who are you and what's your deal?"

She shook her head, eyes darting back and forth between me and Fred. Her next words were an accusation. "You're the girl."

I stepped closer to Fred, wordlessly asking for his protection against the wild-eyed chick. He obligingly put his arm around me, and Jessica's mouth opened like a codfish.

"Oh, my God," she said. "You guys set me up! How did you do it? You looked exactly like her."

I knew who she meant, but Fred asked, "Who?"

She pointed at me. "Penny!"

Fred looked at me and I widened my eyes and lifted my shoulders in an almost imperceptible shrug.

"What are you talking about?" he asked.

"In the woods today. She had, like, a Penny mask on. And it was a damned good one, too, because she had me all convinced she was Penny's freaking ghost."

I bit my lip, slowly lifting my eyebrows to indicate how concerned I was at this strange girl's bizarre accusations.

"Oh, no you don't," Jessica said through teeth now clenched in anger. "You are not going to look at me like I'm crazy and act like you didn't do it!"

A new voice joined the conversation from behind. "What's going on here?"

He was speaking with an American accent, but I recognized Seamus' voice before I turned and saw him. He sent, *I'm your father*.

I sent back, *I'm Tory*, before exclaiming, "Dad!"

I didn't have to pretend to be happy to see him. "This is Fred. And…" I looked at Jessica.

She said, "Right. Like you don't know. Whatever, freaks."

To my relief she stalked off towards Ravenous.

Introducing yourself to the new girlfriend's parent is an awkward situation under the best of circumstances, but Fred had to contend with Jessica's apparent nonsense, too. He handled it well, I thought, stepping toward Seamus with hand extended, saying simply, "Sir."

Seamus shook his hand. His new face was older and courser than the one I was used to. His normally large and aquiline nose was now wide and bulbous, like that of a lifelong drinker. He had a half-inch of grizzled stubble on his chin and deep furrows in his forehead and alongside his mouth. Overall, I got the impression of a stern fishing boat captain with a short fuse and an absent sense of humor.

"It's nice to meet you, Fred." Whatever else he was going to say was interrupted by a loud burst of music from his pocket. He winced, probably at Higgins' choice of ring-tone, the Star Wars theme, but pulled the phone out of his pocket and glanced at the display.

It's a text from Higgins, he sent.

To give me an excuse to see the text that Higgins sent to his own phone, I stepped close alongside him and said for Fred's benefit, "Is it Mom?"

The text read: Urgent! Watch vid. Higgs.

To Fred, Seamus said, "Excuse us a moment," and we both moved several feet away before he tapped the screen with his thumb. A video began to play.

On screen was a man I'd never seen before. He wore a grey suit and had sparse, combed-over blonde hair. His thin lips and receding chin hardly moved when he spoke in a clipped British accent.

"Jolly good work, agent Collins. Too bad about the samples, but the footage got us the go-ahead to take the op to the next level. Hennesy's team will pick up Mum once she's off shift. Surveil the house in the meantime; the subjects might attempt to get her to safety. All entrances and exits covered; disable phone and cable. Only family enters or exits. No obvious casualties—we don't want local authorities involved this time—but if compromised, neutralize the family. Do not underestimate these creatures. Assume nothing and be ready for anything."

The video ended there.

They're talking about Mom! I sent. My empty stomach clenched with fear.

Seamus lifted one bushy eyebrow, which I took as agreement that my mom was indeed the 'Mum' referred to in the video. He replayed it, but I couldn't watch again.

I wanted to cry; wanted to scream. The relative ease of our escape had lulled me into a false sense of security. From the moment Seamus had confirmed these people might go after my mom, I was terrified for her in an abstract, 'what if?' sort of way. Now it was a reality.

With the phones to the Spencer household disabled, I wouldn't be able to call and warn her. And with the house under surveillance, the only way to get a message to her would be if I asked Fred to do it. But if something went wrong, if Mr. Collins and his goons figured out what we were doing, Fred and his family would be 'neutralized.'

I couldn't just sit by and let these monsters kidnap my mom. I thought about the tray of hypodermic needles. What if they wanted to perform horrible experiments on her? I'd escaped with Seamus' help, but who knows what they would have done to us? Mom wasn't a shapeshifter, but they would assume she was, since she was my mother and I'd so foolishly given myself away when Mr. Collins had seen a dead girl walking. Seeing Penny like that, he would have known immediately I was one of them, but if I hadn't confirmed who I was by saying, "Mr. Collins!" like a tool, he wouldn't have known for sure Tainie Strauss was really me.

This was all my fault.

I'd actually forgotten Fred until he came over and said softly, "Bad news?"

"You might say that." The words were barely audible. My fear left me breathless. I hardly noticed when he put his arm around me.

It wasn't as if I had several courses of action to choose from. There was only one way to save Mom and keep Fred safe at the same time.

I leaned away from him and forced a smile.

"How's Stephen?"

"My brother? To be honest…he's in jail."

"What for?" As if I didn't know.

"It's bogus. Well, the drunk-driving charge isn't, but he wouldn't have been drunk if the cops didn't think he…hurt…his ex-girlfriend Penny, the girl Jessica just—whatever she just accused you of. None of it makes any sense and this whole thing is ripping my mom up."

"What if I told you I could find out what really happened to Penny?" It was a bold, bald statement, but I was suddenly sure I could do it. With Mom's life potentially on the line, I could do anything. Even if it would ruin my chances for any kind of relationship with Fred.

Seamus stepped into view, a deep frown on his face. Aloud, he said, "We've got to get going, honey," while the words *What are you saying*? rang in my mind.

"Okay, Daddy." *We need him*! *I know how we can save Mom*!

When Fred said, "Wait a minute. How?" it took me a moment to get my conversations straight.

"It's complicated," I replied, shooting Seamus a silently pleading look. "And first, there's something I need to tell you."

Seamus took a moment to assess Fred, with his clean-cut looks and honest, open face, before looking back into my eyes. *Trust is a dangerous thing.*

Do you have any better ideas?

Chapter Twenty-six

There's no easy way to tell someone you're a shapeshifter.

Although Seamus thought bringing Fred into the situation could only end badly, he reluctantly agreed to wait in the car he'd rented while Fred and I talked. Convincing Seamus my plan had merit was cake compared to what I faced with Fred.

Stephen's blue mustang was parked under a light pole that was partially buried under dirty chunks of snow.

"It's my brother's car," he said, opening the passenger door for me.

I sat on the cold seat and tucked my J.C. Penny bag down at my feet. "I know. I saw him get arrested."

Without answering, he shut my door and came around to settle in the driver's seat. He placed his hands on the steering wheel at ten-and-two and locked his elbows, staring out the windshield into the dark parking lot. "I didn't notice you."

I took a deep breath and let it out slowly. "But you have noticed a lot of weird things have been happening lately, right?"

He gave a faint shake of his head. "Like?"

"Like the giant otter? The second General Lee? My—I mean—Tainie Strauss' clothes in the creek?"

He looked wary all of a sudden. "She said someone stole them out of the laundry room. I figured it was you. You must know her."

I am her.

I thought it, and opened my mouth to say it, but the words wouldn't come.

Instead, I blurted, "Her mother's in danger. I need to borrow your car to get Mrs. Strauss out of your house."

I saw—from the blank look that crept over his face—that I'd lost him.

"Uh huh." It was a non-committal 'tell me more, but I already don't believe you' kind of response.

I wished I knew him better. He'd shown me kindness in school, and as Tory, we'd exchanged some spit. But I had no idea if, like Higgins, he was capable of taking what I was about to tell him in stride. If he freaked, would I be able to bump this up to the next level—kick him out of his brother's car, steal it, and pose as Fred to get into his house? I could barely imagine doing so, which meant I'd better convince him to help us, and I'd better do it fast.

"I'm a shapeshifter."

There. I'd said it.

He relaxed his arms, but his hands continued to grip the steering wheel. He didn't turn his head, but the light from the street lamp reflected off his eyes as he slanted them towards me.

"Show me."

My heart skipped a few beats. I'd expected him to come back at me with patent disbelief, not a demand for proof. "Are you sure? Y–you want to see it?"

His head fell back on the headrest with a mild thump and he rolled his eyes to the roof of the car. "No, Tory, I'm just going to take your flipping word for it. What kind of moron do you think I am? What is it with the chicks in my life? I got Jessica stalking me and screaming about seeing ghosts and you, with the drowning-yourself-naked-in-the-creek bullcrap. Oh, and now you're a shapeshifter. So, yeah. I want to see you do it!"

He turned and saw me, and his mouth snapped shut.

While he was busy ranting, I'd briefly debated who to become. Penny got a great reaction out of Jessica, but I felt bad using her likeness, as if it were some kind of desecration. Stephen would be good, but the idea of becoming a guy, with the resulting changes below the belt, did not appeal in the slightest. I didn't want to become myself, because even after everything that had happened, I still couldn't admit who I really was. I settled for someone who'd been front and center in our personal headlines lately.

Jessica waggled her fingers and offered him an apologetic smile.

The silence that followed went on for what felt like forever. I went ahead and read his mind for most of it, since it seemed he was unable to verbalize what was going through it. But the thoughts I picked up were disjointed, like trying to find a good radio station. *Jessica!—that's impossible, no way they could have made the switch—I only looked away for a second and didn't hear a thing—she said she was a shapeshifter—that's impossible—no way—I must be losing my mind—Jessica—the real Jessica—said we played a trick on her—said she saw Penny's ghost—said Tory was wearing a really good mask.*

I knew he was going to reach out before his hands grabbed my face.

He pushed and pulled and twisted my skin like it was putty, like he hoped it was putty, until I said, "Ouch!"

He was breathing so hard the windows began to fog up. His disbelief was a heavy presence in the small car. "Show me to my face," he said. "I want to see you do it."

"Who should I be?" I asked softly. The young man who'd fought the raging current of the creek to rescue me and who carried me through the cold wind and rain without effort seemed fragile to me now. I felt like a major jerk for doing this to him. Then I thought of Mom and steeled myself against the sympathy. He'd get over it.

"Tainie," he demanded. "Be Tainie."

My own face.

I'd watched myself change in the mirror, so I wasn't surprised at Fred's reaction when he witnessed it: a mix of fascinated horror, disbelief and awe. After the change, I let him paw my face again, but only for a few seconds before I changed back into Tory. It wasn't fair of me to think it, but I couldn't help wondering how much of the "horror" of his reaction was from seeing me become my ugly self. Not that he knew Tainie was the real me, and the more I thought about it, the more I was determined he never would.

"This is insane." He sounded almost defeated.

I nodded in enthusiastic agreement. "It is. It's nuts. I only just found out about it, so you won't get any argument from me. But now there're these bad guys after us, and they're going to kidnap Mrs. Strauss in order to get to us."

"Why? And who's 'us?' Your dad?"

I noticed he was leaning against the car door about as far away from me as physically possible. I tried to smile reassuringly.

"He isn't really my dad, but, yeah. He's like me."

"Mrs. Strauss, too?"

"No, she's…" I didn't want to say 'human.' "She's normal."

"Why would they kidnap her?"

I'd hoped he wouldn't ask that, because a logical lie hadn't occurred to me yet. Luckily, a rap on the driver's side window that made Fred jump saved me from having to wing an explanation. Seamus bent at the waist to look into the car, still in the guise of my 'dad.' Fred rolled down the window.

"Have we got an understanding?" Seamus asked.

I leaned over, ignoring how Fred pressed himself back into the seat to avoid contact with me, and said, "We hadn't gotten that far."

"Well we'd best work out the details soon." Seamus reached across

Fred to hand me Higgins' phone. The words on the screen said, "You were right. I'm expendable. Exit stage left."

"That's cryptic," I said.

"Let's hope he got away. He took a risk sending that video."

"What video?" Fred asked.

I looked at Seamus. *If we show it to him, it will explain a lot.*

He gave a short nod, and I played the video for Fred. After the last words faded away he asked in a stunned voice, "How do you 'neutralize' someone without getting the cops involved?"

"Make it look like an accident," Seamus replied.

"This is messed up." Fred's voice was thick, like he was fighting back tears. The dim light inside the car didn't hide the curl of his lip when he looked at me. Sheer hate is hard to mistake; it took my breath away.

Of course he'd hate me now—I brought the roof down on him and his whole family. The fact that I didn't deserve it didn't make it sting any less.

Seamus opened the door and climbed into the back seat. "We don't have time for recrimination. Do you have a map of the area?"

Fred gestured to the glove box and I found a map inside. He stared out the window while Seamus unfolded it and I turned on the overhead light.

"Okay, here's the house. We can't know how many agents will be involved, but if it were my op, I'd put someone here, here and here at the very least." He poked his finger at the map. "They don't want to attract attention, so they've probably got people in vehicles."

I pointed to a wedge of green. "These are the condos where Mrs. Strauss lives. This is the park. She walks this way, through these woods."

"It's the obvious route, and they are likely to have someone waiting. Fred, you and Tory take my rental and park here." Fred hesitated, but finally turned from the window and glanced at the map.

Seamus said, "I'll go in as you and smuggle Sophie out. If something goes wrong, I will do everything in my power to protect your family. Tory, this is important. I'm ninety-nine percent certain their goal is to get us to lure Caitlin out of hiding."

"Who's Caitlin?" Fred asked.

I didn't know how to explain Caitlin. The truth, that she was the last of the ancient shapeshifter royalty, in possession of the gossamer crown, sounded melodramatic. Seamus summed it up with a simple, "She has something they want."

"Oh, no," I murmured, remembering the phone call from the woman who'd claimed to be Seamus' partner. She'd asked us to find Caitlin, but Mom suspected it was a ploy to lure her out of hiding. Now I knew why.

"They want the crown."

"What's the crown?" Fred sounded impatient.

"It's best you have as little knowledge of it as possible in the event that you are questioned in future," Seamus replied.

"Whatever." Fred went back to looking out the window, jaw clenched. "I don't understand why we just don't call the damn police."

"And tell them what?" Seamus said.

Fred didn't answer. I knew he was running the possible scenarios through his mind and coming up with the likelihood that even without the shapeshifter aspect, the police would respond with skepticism at best.

"If this doesn't work," I said to Seamus, "How do I contact Caitlin?"

Seamus frowned and began shaking his head. "I have absolutely no idea."

Chapter Twenty-seven

Even though the back seat of Seamus' rented Ford Focus was cramped, Fred still managed to avoid touching me. Despite the tinted back windows, I felt exposed and kept glancing away from Fred's house to scan the area for evidence of lurking agents. We were parked a block away and around the corner, but had a good view of the front of the house. It was well lit. Apparently Old Lady Spencer had installed spotlights to show off the row of white columns that gave the estate its regal old-world appearance.

"You've got that phone, right?" he asked.

"Yeah."

"We could call the police right now, and if something does happen, they'll already be on their way."

"You don't think the agents have police scanners?"

He compressed his lips and looked back at the house. After a while he took a breath and said, "You know, my grandparents are a pain, but I love them. And I'd do anything for my mom."

"She's lucky to have you."

We'd driven behind Seamus from a distance, parked, and watched as 'Fred' drove Stephen's Mustang up to the house, opened the garage door and disappeared inside. He had a note to hand to my Mom. It said, "Don't say anything! I'm not Fred. It's Seamus. Will explain later, but must get you out. Come with me and DO NOT REACT. We are being watched. Family is in danger."

It hadn't even been ten minutes. Who knows how long it would take false Fred to get Mom alone?

Out of the blue, Fred said, "Show me again."

"What?"

"Change into something not human this time. I'm starting to think this is some kind of crazy scheme. Maybe you and your dad are planning to kidnap my mom."

He was panicking; I saw it in his eyes and didn't blame him one iota.

"I can do it, but I have to take off my clothes or else they'll tear or strangle me."

He made a scoffing laugh. "I've seen you naked before. It's no big."

It was intended as an insult. He seemed unmoved by the hurt on my face, saying only, "Do it now, or I swear I'll get out of this car."

A deep sigh escaped me as I removed my coat. I hadn't had a chance to practice shapeshifting into any animals other than the otter and General Lee. If I went with the dog, I could keep my shirt on, at least. I toed off my boots, unbuttoned my jeans and pulled them down past my hips.

Suddenly Fred lunged for me, grasping me under the arms and lifting me partially onto his lap so quickly I didn't have time to protest. His kiss was totally unexpected. After all the grief he'd given me, I knew there was no way the sight of me shimmying out of my pants had set him on fire.

Which meant someone was outside looking in. A quick scan of Fred's mind confirmed it. He'd seen a crouching, dark-clothed figure move out from behind the car across the street and head straight for us.

I wrapped my arms around him and kissed him back, trying to put on a show for the intruder. Fred slid one hand down and cupped my backside while the other went under my shirt. I wanted to protest—he didn't have to take such liberties just to prove we were really going at it—did he? But the sensation of his hand stroking my skin disengaged me from the real reason we were in each other's arms. I couldn't control myself, what started out as a stiff response changed into something else entirely. My body melted against his, and I felt him arch his back to get closer to me. Our mouths fused together. He tugged my jeans away from my lower legs and eased me fully onto his lap. I straddled him, engulfed in the conflagration.

To say what happened next was like being doused with a bucket of cold water would be less of a cliché and more of an understatement.

We jumped apart at a piercing drawn-out screech of tires on pavement. I whipped my head around just in time to see the Mustang, with one occupant hunched over the steering wheel, race down the street in front of us, followed closely by two sedans. A man, probably the same one we'd been putting on a show for, sprinted toward a white van coming our way. While I sat there with my mouth open, the sliding side door of the van opened, giving us a glimpse of the equipment in the interior. The man leapt inside and the van shot off in the same direction as Seamus.

Fred reached for the door handle, but I grabbed his arm. "Wait!"

"No!" He yanked his arm away. "I have to check on my Mom."

I knew exactly how he felt, but what if the bad guys were in his house? He had the door partially open, but I gripped his coat and hung on, preventing him from exiting.

"Get off me!" He shoved me so hard I fell back against the far door and smacked my head on the window. I could only watch helplessly as he got out. The echo of the slamming door hadn't faded before a lone tear traced its way down my cheek. I sat in the cold car as he ran across the street, up his driveway and disappeared behind the front door. No one accosted him.

Seamus, who may or may not have carried out enough of the plan to get my mom stashed in the back of Stephen Spencer's car, was gone. If Mom was still in the house, Fred would surely tell her what was going on and she'd come to me.

I waited.

No more cars shot by; no more dark-clothed figures approached, and not so much as a light went on at Fred's house.

I didn't know what to do, but one thing was certain: the Spencer house was off-limits. Fred hated my guts now and I had no way of knowing if the agents had left anyone behind to continue surveillance.

I didn't dare go home to Gramma Foster's. I couldn't drive, but even if I had taken Driver's Ed, Fred had the rental car keys in his pocket. We were supposed to have waited until we'd seen Seamus leave the house in the Mustang and then follow him. There was no plan B. All Seamus had said was, "If this doesn't work, get far away and hide." He said it almost matter-of-factly, as if leaving everything he knew at a moment's notice was a commonplace event in his life.

Moving slowly, I changed into my new clothes and stuffed the old ones into the bag, ashamed that I'd let my passion for Fred overshadow common sense. Not that things would have happened differently had I witnessed the first few seconds of Seamus' escape.

I wondered what the chances were that he and my mom had gotten away and realized I already knew. They hadn't. Maybe Seamus alone could have done it, but Mom was a liability. And odds were good Mr. Collins, *agent* Collins, would have already changed locations from the house Seamus and I had been kept to somewhere…well…I'd never find it, anyway.

I rubbed the back of my head where I'd cracked it on the window. It didn't hurt really, except for my feelings. I hoped rather pathetically that Fred would ascertain his mother was fine and come back out. That he wouldn't leave me sitting here stewing in my fear and doubt. At the same time, I suspected the longer I sat here, the more likely it was that the bad guys would catch me.

What I wouldn't have given at that moment to be home in bed, to be ugly Tainie Strauss again.

Chapter Twenty-eight

Higgins' phone told me exactly how much time had passed. I waited one hour to the minute before deciding it was time for me to go. There was still over a hundred dollars from the money Seamus had given me in my pocket. Philadelphia was a big city and since I had the ability to hide in plain sight, I wouldn't have to spend that money fleeing to another town. Jobs were hard to come by, but I was sure there were plenty of opportunities for a shapeshifter to support herself—the dishonest way. I'd have to think of some way to safely contact Gramma Foster and let her know how Mom could find me when (I refused to consider that it might be 'if') she looked for me.

As much as I wanted to walk past Fred's house, give him one last chance to rush out and tell me he was sorry, I knew better. That was my heart talking; my head reminded me not only that I was still in danger, but that Fred despised and probably feared me. He was in that house with his family, appreciating them like never before. Before long, he would convince himself that what he'd seen hadn't been real.

As I got out of the car I remembered how I felt like the loneliest girl on earth only a few days ago. I guess there's no such thing as rock bottom; life erodes and chisels away even the hardest rock and we can always get lower.

Hands stuffed deep in my pockets, I walked in the opposite direction of Fred's house, fighting the urge to look back. It was late, but the neighborhood was far from asleep. From more than one house I heard music or talking or the sound of a blaring television laugh track. It was Friday night and even in the post-Cataclysm world, families were enjoying each others' company. It had only ever been Mom and me, but that had always been enough. She taught me to be pragmatic, but I doubted she had this situation in mind.

I had to think of a way to get my life back.

In case anyone looked out and saw me trudging by, I tried to look like I had a destination. The air was frigid cold, and every shadow menaced. The street lights may have been plentiful in such an affluent neighborhood, but there were also a lot of bushes and stone fences and wrought-iron gates that could shield someone from view. I expected one of Collins' goons to jump out at me from every cranny.

I'd walked several blocks, completely lost as I zig-zagged from street to street, when I sensed I was being followed. A furtive glance behind me verified it; someone tall was there, walking briskly toward me about half a block away. I turned to face front, barely stopping myself from running full-bore in any direction. There was a good chance this person was out for an evening stroll, but I didn't think so. Maybe it was that Irish intuition.

A house, I thought. If I banged on the front door of a random house, I could beg the occupants for help.

The houses on this block weren't nearly as nice as the ones near the Spencer property. The dark night, coupled with my own dark thoughts, had kept me from realizing I'd strayed into a lower-income area. Still, any help was better than no help. I heard my follower's footsteps now and turned up the nearest walkway. The house looked deserted, but the door was only seconds away.

I didn't make it.

My pursuer barely laid a hand on my shoulder before I exploded with a shrill scream.

"Tory!"

I went from terrified to angry in zero seconds flat, whirling around and whacking Fred in the side of the head with my open hand.

"You scared the hell out of me!"

For good measure I whapped him a few more times, until he grabbed my hands and forced my arms behind my back. Instantly, I burst into tears.

To my undying gratitude, his restraining hold on me changed to an embrace. I pressed my forehead against his jacket and felt him bury his face in my hair.

My mom always told me it's better to not do something in the first place than to have to apologize afterwards. That didn't make the two sweet words he uttered, "I'm sorry," any less effective. Fred could have gotten anything from me at that moment.

With a monumental effort, I choked back my tears. As easy as it would be to relinquish control and sob my heart out, standing in some stranger's front yard in the middle of the night was neither the place nor time. "Did my mom get away?"

"She wasn't in the house."

"And your family?"

"No sign of any agents. My mom was asleep and my grandparents are both sloppy drunk, but that's not unusual. I gotta tell you, the word 'neutralize' will never be the same for me after this."

A short, humorless laugh escaped me. Just as I started to think he'd gotten over the shock and no longer hated me, he pulled the rental car key out of his pocket and handed it to me.

"Oh," I said. "Thanks."

But then, instead of walking away, he said, "I guess you can't go home. Is there anyone safe you can stay with?"

I shook my head and held up the key. It reflected the light from the streetlamp. "I don't even know how to drive."

He took the key back with no hesitation. "Alright, let's go find you a motel. I know a place that takes cash and doesn't ask questions."

I gave him a suspicious look and he explained with one word: "Stephen."

"Ah."

We walked past several houses. He didn't try to hold my hand or put his arm around me and I didn't have the courage to read his mind to verify those days were gone forever. We were on our way to a motel together, but I wasn't exactly overcome with excitement. There was nothing romantic or clandestine about it. Still, the fact that he'd come after me, even if only to give me back the rental key, was enough to lift my spirits. A little.

My thoughts kept swinging back around to my mom. If she and Seamus had gotten away, she'd be worried sick about me. If they didn't, she'd still be worried sick. Either scenario, I had no way of reassuring her I was alright.

"What if you became Tainie?" Fred asked out of the blue.

"What?"

He stopped on the sidewalk in front of a house that still had Christmas decorations in the unkempt yard. Half buried in the snow, a big plastic candy cane leaned forlornly against the wire frame of a light-up reindeer.

"You could stay here tonight. This is where Tainie's friend Gina's lives. I know because this was my grandparent's house before they won the lottery and now they rent it out."

So that's why Gina didn't like Fred! His family were the evil overlords. Then a vague memory surfaced: Gina in the lunchroom talking about her sister who was involved with a group of people—what had she said? Something about a whole movement of folks who thought the cataclysm was no act of nature. I'd initially dismissed it as nonsense, but now I knew better. Maybe, just maybe, these people actually knew something useful that might lead me to Caitlin.

"Do you think she'd let Tainie stay?"

"Worth a try, right? Tell her your pipes burst and flooded your house or something. Then you'll be right around the corner from me so tomorrow you can do whatever you have in mind to help find Penny's real killer."

Oh. That.

Chapter Twenty-nine

Gina answered the door.

"Whoa! What are *you* guys doing here?"

I was Tainie again, of course. "I need your help."

"Well, come on in!" She waved her hand like a game show host.

"Are your parents home?" Fred asked.

She gave him a look; a half stymied, half contemptuous you-should-know-the-answer-to-that-question look. "I only have the one parent, and she works the late shift at McDonalds. Before the Cataclysm, she and my dad were zookeepers."

I was so grateful for the warmth inside the house that it took me a moment to realize the significance of what she said. From what she'd told us in class, her family used to live in Tampa, Florida.

The undersea volcanic eruptions that plagued the Pacific Ring of Fire during the Cataclysm had temporarily raised ocean temperatures worldwide, resulting in a rough and fierce mid-point to the hurricane season. A category five monster had curved like a scythe across the Gulf of Mexico two weeks after the Cataclysm had been declared officially over and slammed into central Florida. It devastated the bulk of the state and completely destroyed the Tampa zoo. Very few of the zoo's animal inhabitants survived, and the minimal staff that stayed to care for them under shelter of the supposedly reinforced buildings also perished.

"Oh, no," I said softly. "Did your father..?"

Gina shook her head angrily, but I knew it was to hide the betraying quiver of her bottom lip. "Yeah, well, it was eight months ago. At least I'm not an orphan, right?"

Fred seemed not to understand, and I didn't bother to enlighten him—Gina clearly didn't want to talk about it. Mom always said the barbed-wire fences people erect around themselves are not just to keep people out, but to keep our feelings from getting out.

The house was a one-story rambler, and its age and smell reminded me of the place Seamus and I had been kept in. Although what I'd seen of that house had been minimally furnished and clean; this place looked like it had recently hosted a frat party that got out of hand. Piles of newspapers, magazines, books and paper littered every surface. My view of the kitchen showed tilting stacks of pots and pans, cups and dishes. From the faint odor of stale garlic and sour milk, I doubted they were clean.

Gina turned into the living room and said matter-of-factly, "I'd ask you to pardon the mess, but this is how it always looks."

Two cats ran into the room. A fat orange tabby went straight for Fred's leg and began sniffing it intently, while a grey tabby with a long, unusually skinny tail rubbed the corner of its mouth against my leg. I stooped to run my hand down its sleek fur. It arched its back, purring unevenly, like an outboard engine with seaweed wrapped around the propeller.

"That's Queenie," Gina said, referring to the grey cat. "Watch out—she bites. She thinks it's how she's supposed to show affection, I guess. The other one is…well, his name is Fred. Coincidence, I swear."

Fred the human looked pleased. "Hey, Fred. Nice name."

The cat ignored him and continued to press its nose against his pant leg.

"Do you have a dog?" Gina asked. "He's not usually so obnoxious."

"Heh, yeah, I guess you could say I have a dog."

"Disguised as a horse," I put in.

Gina apparently had enough chit-chat. "So why are you guys here? Together? It's kinda late."

I fed her the line about the burst pipes, expecting her to come back with a million questions poking holes in the logic of me requesting to stay with her, but she said, "Alright, you can sleep on the couch—if you can find it under all the crap."

She looked pointedly at Fred, and to my surprise, he said, "We're trying to solve Penny's murder. Can we use your notebook?"

Her eyes behind the thick lenses squinted suspiciously. "Don't you have a computer? You live in a mansion."

"Our phone, Internet and cable are out at the moment," he replied.

It was true, but Gina would never know why. She lifted her eyebrows and said, "This way."

Off a narrow hallway, she led us into a room furnished with a twin captain's bed in solid honey oak, a matching dresser and a desk. The neatness of her bedroom was in stark contrast to the rest of the house. I noticed there was nothing on the walls—no posters or pictures, nor had there been any hanging elsewhere in the house, come to think of it.

She must have noticed me looking at the walls. "We're renting. The owners didn't want nail holes in the wallboard."

Fred ignored the snarky reference to his grandparents.

Gina sat in a white plastic patio chair at the desk. Her little notebook was already open and connected to the Internet.

"What do you need?" Her fingers hovered over the keyboard.

I had no idea where to begin in the investigation of Penny's murder. The whole idea had been a rash promise designed to get Fred to cooperate, and it was based on the fact that I could become anyone I wanted. I'd had the vague notion I could ask questions of suspects without them realizing who they were really talking to. That would work just fine if I knew what to ask, who to ask, and who to be when I asked.

Gina was waiting for an answer, but I had no idea where to start. I did, however, have something else I needed to know, so I decided to take another tack.

"Well, um…remember how you told me your sister had friends who thought the Cataclysm was caused by…uh, magic or something? And you showed me that website with the picture of Seamus the Bard?"

"Yeah. What's that got to do with Penny?"

Fred, too, looked at me quizzically. I thought it best to sound nonchalant as I lied. "Maybe nothing, but I saw a strange man the other day, hanging around the complex. He reminded me of that bard guy."

The skeptical look was still firmly in place on her face, so I added lamely, "It really looked like him."

Fred couldn't possibly know I was making it all up, but he took the reins. "It's the only lead we have. Right now my brother's in jail and the cops are trying to get him to confess to something I know he didn't do. They aren't even investigating anyone else."

"Huh. Alright, well, whatever you say." She began tapping rapidly on her keyboard.

"Here," she said. "This is the website I showed you, What Caused the Cataclysm dot com. Mostly it's articles from scientists trying to explain what happened—nobody can agree on anything of course. But it also covers alternate theories, with arguments for and against things like Armageddon and magic and stuff."

She clicked on a link that said 'Prophets,' and then on the link 'Seamus the Bard.'

There was one small paragraph. "The url to Seamus the Bard's website is no longer valid. The site was originally dedicated to The Bard's (real name/identity unknown) stories and legends out of ancient Ireland regarding the Fae or the Folk, who were, according to him, shapeshifters.

Before the Cataclysm began, The Bard was one of the first people to warn his readership that the modern world was in dire danger. In the last days of the Cataclysm he asked his followers (purported to be descended from shapeshifters themselves, as was The Bard) to meet him in London to help stop the destruction. Soon after, the anomalies causing disturbances in the earth's magnetic field and all abnormal movement of the earth's crust completely ceased. Coincidence?"

"That's it?" I asked.

Gina hit the back button on her browser. "Pretty much. It's like these guys came out of hiding, saved the world, and disappeared. If you believe that sort of thing, and to be honest, I think it's just as valid an explanation as what the scientists came up with."

She sounded defensive and I suppressed the urge to tell her I believed it, too; could prove it, in fact.

She was about to click another link when Fred said, "Wait! What's that?"

It was a picture of a young Asian man with spiked-up hair, wearing a big sign that said, 'The End is Near.'

Gina clicked on it. "Oh, yeah, I saw that guy before. He posted a video on YouTube before the Cataclysm that went viral afterward."

"I saw it," Fred said. "It was that video warning San Francisco the Big One was coming. Everyone thought he was a lunatic but then it happened just like he said. Did you see it, Tory?"

I gave him a look that would wither all the snakes on Medusa's head. "My name is Tainie, thank you very much. And no, I never saw it. I was too busy fleeing during the Cataclysm." And unwittingly participating in the ceremony to stop it.

Gina clicked on a link.

"Oh, you gotta see it. His name is Zach Wong." She frowned at the screen. "…aaaaand the link to the video isn't working." She uttered a little "grrrrr" sound and went to Google, typing some criteria in the search box. After clicking on several possibilities, she said, "Looks like the vid's been taken down, but here's another picture of him. Cute, huh?"

"Oh, yeah, he's adorable." Fred's voice was like dry ice.

"Wasn't asking you."

The photo was posted on the San Francisco Police Department website, of all places. It wasn't a mugshot, but was included with pictures of new recruits participating in some sort of community outreach.

"He's a cop?" I asked.

"I guess so."

Fred leaned in for a better look. "What's he got—a crow on his shoulder?"

Looking at the photo of the large black bird with eerie blue eyes perched on a smiling Zach Wong's shoulder, I had a sudden memory. Back on the ship, in the middle of the North Sea, I'd been so sick at one point I imagined I'd heard the raucous cawing of a raven.

Gina started to say something, but a sharp sound startled us all, and for a disorienting second, I thought I was hearing the raven again. But it was Higgins' phone, blaring music.

I met Fred's eyes, unsure what to do.

"Answer it," he said.

I pulled it from my pocket and looked at the display, not that any numbers that might appear there would be familiar to me.

"Answer it," Fred said again. "It might be your dad."

I tapped my finger on the 'answer' button and said, "H-hello?"

"Is this Tainie?" The voice was loud over the background noise of what sounded like an overtaxed engine, like the caller was in a speeding car. For a brief, shining moment, I thought it really was Seamus—thought they were still on the run, still free.

"Yes!"

"It's Higgs! I'm sending you a file with names on it. Don't forward it to anyone, just open it and copy the names down and ditch my cell phone! Did you get that?" Higgins' voice had risen to a shout.

"Where's my mom?" I yelled into the phone.

"Get the names, ditch the cell!"

The call ended abruptly. From Fred and Gina's concerned faces, it was clear they'd heard the entire conversation.

"What's going on?" Gina asked. "Where is your mother?"

Tears flooded my eyes. I rolled them to the ceiling and blinked a few times. Fred took the phone out of my hand as Gina repeated, "What's going on? The truth would be nice."

I took a steadying breath and said, "I'd very much like to tell you the truth, but half the time, I'm not even sure what it is. Mom's…missing. And–"

"Just type these names, okay?" Fred cut me off, which was a good thing, since I didn't know how much I could reveal without compromising Gina's safety, too. It had finally sunk in that anyone who helped me would be in potential danger.

"Fine," Gina said with a huff. Fred began rattling off names in alphabetical order, none of which sounded familiar. He read them quickly, but Gina was a fast typist. When they came to the name 'Caitlin O'Connor,' I gasped.

Fred looked up from Higgins' cell phone. "What?"

"That—that's Caitlin!"

"It's just a name, Tory," he replied. "There's nothing but names on this list—no information on how to find her."

"Why do you keep calling her Tory?" Gina asked.

"Sorry. Tainie."

Without waiting for her to ask further questions, he recited another name. Gina dutifully typed it. I wondered how much of her cooperation had to do with Fred's presence. If it were just me, she'd be tossing the questions out like grenades and not accepting my non-answers.

When Fred read, "Sophie Strauss. Titania Strauss," Gina only glanced up at me.

The last name on the list was 'Zach Wong.' My ability to be surprised at anything at that point was sorely stretched. Seamus the Bard and Zach Wong were both included on a website that listed all the factors and contributors the webmaster could find, both logical and fantastical, as to the causes of the Cataclysm. For all I knew, the list of names Higgins sent me had been at least partially compiled from the information on that website.

"Wait a minute," Gina said in a tone that told me we'd finally reached the end of her patience. "Are we talking the same Zach Wong? You guys really need to tell me what's going on."

Fred turned on her. "Does it sound like we have time to give you a detailed rundown? We have to figure out what to do with the list of names and get rid of this cell phone before…" he looked at me for the answer just as it dawned on me.

"Before they trace it to us," I said quietly, a rush of fear flooding my system.

Gina wasn't satisfied. "And 'they' are..?"

"Bad guys," Fred said shortly.

For the first time that night, Gina had the proper look of concern behind her eyes and I felt like a complete jerk for putting it there. I headed for her bedroom door.

"I didn't mean to drag you into this, Gina. And Fred, we have to get out of here, and you need to go home. I'm sorry, but until things settle down I won't be able to help you figure out what happened to Penny."

He grabbed my arm. "I already know what happened to her. You think her death is a coincidence? No, Tainie—it *is* Tainie, isn't it? She was in the wrong place at the wrong time. They were after you."

Chapter Thirty

In spite of my lies and attempts at evasion, open-minded Gina still managed to home in on the truth.

"You're one of them, aren't you?"

Fred let go of my arm and patted me on the back, very un-boyfriend like. It penetrated: he knew I wasn't Tory.

"Just tell her," he said.

I didn't know how much time we had, but the jig was clearly up, so I took a deep breath and told them both everything I knew. It took longer than I thought it would, and not just because Gina kept lobbing question-grenades at me. I had to clear up Fred's misconceptions from the lies I'd told him. And there were still so many things I didn't understand myself—which made it all that much harder to put into words. The only thing I held back was the mind-reading part. I didn't want them to be any more uncomfortable around me than absolutely necessary.

When we reached the part where Gina wanted to see me shift, I did it without hesitation. For the first time since I'd accepted that I was vastly different from everyone around me, I felt…I don't know…almost ashamed. Or maybe I was just exhausted. By the time I slipped out of my pants and changed into General Lee it was very late and I was asleep on my paws.

I'd forgotten about Gina's cats, which had wandered into the bedroom at some point and were snoozing on her bed. Barking as part of my demonstration probably wasn't my most brilliant move of the evening. The two cats leapt high into the air and I laughed, which came out sounding like a series of coughing growls that didn't help matters. The cats rebounded back up off the mattress. Queenie landed all-claws-out in the curtains, while feline-Fred twisted in mid-air and bounced onto the floor. He made a break for the door, but since I was blocking it, he arched his back and hissed furiously, boinging like a spring on straight, stiff legs before shooting under the bed.

Gina was laughing hysterically, but she managed to say, "Change back! Change back!"

I became Tory, and decided to stay that way.

While I put on my pants and Fred tried to get Queenie out of the curtains, Gina paced back and forth, waving her hands in the air and verbally attempting to get a handle on everything.

"This is…amazing! It's…I can't even…wow! I mean…I knew the Cataclysm wasn't natural! I can't wait to talk to your mom and find out exactly why. I can't believe you—scientific Tainie—didn't want to find out more. Well, okay, yeah, I get that you thought your mom was loonie-bins, but as soon as you shifted that very first time you should have been a believer with a capital B!"

She stopped in front of me and said, "You're beautiful. God, I wish I could do that."

I thought about the state of my life, thought about mentioning that she wouldn't be able to talk to my mom any time soon, and replied, "It doesn't fix everything."

She opened her mouth, probably to argue with me, but a sound from outside stopped her. Fred's hand, which had been soothing Queenie's ruffled fur, stilled. I held my breath.

Another sound; this time I made out a muffled male voice swearing.

"They're in the backyard," Gina whispered. "Tripping over the junk buried under the snow."

"Right," Fred said quietly. He stood and brushed past me into the hall where he looked up at the ceiling. "Up into the attic—hurry!"

He grasped a dangling pull rope and heaved on it. A ladder slid down, long unused hinges creaking and wooden boards grating against each other.

"Like they're not going to look up there," Gina whispered. She sat quickly at her desk and tapped on the keys.

"What are you doing?" I asked.

"Taking out some insurance," she said through clenched teeth.

Fred said, "You forget this used to be my grandparent's house. They only finished part of the attic. There's a great place to hide up there. Come on!"

He shooed me up the rickety stairs as Gina continued to type. He hissed, "So help me, Gina, if you don't get your–"

"I'm coming!" I heard her whisper loudly. The attic above me was black as a cave. As I ascended I tried not to think about spiders, but almost immediately upon entering the place I encountered a web. I swiped at my face and stepped aside for Fred and Gina. There were dusty, abandoned boxes stacked everywhere. My knee tipped one over and I barely caught it before it crashed down, but not before half the contents spilled out. I stuffed the moth-bally old suit jackets back in and closed the box flap.

Someone knocked on the door and for a moment, we all froze in place.

"Like we're just going to let them in," Fred muttered, pushing Gina from behind.

Once we were all safely up, he pulled the ladder up. "We need to get settled and hold as still as possible. If the rafters squeak, it will give us away in a heartbeat."

I didn't know how he could see anything in the faint light that seeped in from around the opening, but I heard a slight scraping as he moved something aside. His hand on my head guided me down through a narrow opening in the wall. As I squeezed myself against the unfinished roof, another knock sounded on the door, this one more forceful than the last. *Bang bang bang bang!*

Scuffling sounds heralded first Gina, then Fred as they joined me in the hidey-space. There was no light whatsoever, but I knew when he slid the cover back into place over the opening, because the exterior sounds became muffled.

"Sit down," he whispered. "We might be here for a while."

I did as he suggested even though the cramped space forced my knees up against my chest. I felt Gina's thigh press up against mine as she did the same. A two-by-four stud pressed uncomfortably into my back and an icy cold draft seeped up from gaps in the floor below. I was almost as scared of this place as I was of the intruders. Almost.

We didn't have long to wait. A muted *Boom!* which I was pretty sure was the sound of the front door getting kicked in, shook the house. Gina flinched next to me and I closed my eyes against the blackness. Fred let out a long, slow, "shhhhhhhh."

Then stomping, and shouting: "Clear!...Clear!" just like on television when the cops went room to room, guns drawn, looking for criminals. Moments later, the sound of the attic ladder going down reached us. I didn't know about Fred and Gina, but I held my breath as the searcher came up and started knocking boxes all about. I never heard a more welcome word as, "Clear!"

They settled in the room below us; Gina's room. I listened intently, but was able to make out only every other word or so. They found her notebook and noticed it was still warm, which led them to become suspicious of the cats. Next to me, Gina gasped as we heard an unmistakable meow of pain. I was frightened for her kitties, but part of me filed away the fact that they didn't know about the size restriction of shifting.

More stomping and a louder voice said clearly, "Where's the cell? The locator puts it here somewhere."

Someone answered, but I couldn't make out what they said.

"Then call the damned thing!" I recognized the voice: Mr. Collins.

My mouth dropped open in horror. Higgins' cell phone was in my pocket. I risked a whisper, "Guys?"

Fred's hand touched my face, and he breathed, "Give it to me!"

Every second that passed while I attempted to find the opening to my coat pocket seemed like a lifetime. I finally pulled the cell phone free and got it into Fred's hand. A moment later, unbearably bright light filled the space. Fred held the display inches from his face, so I saw his expression: confusion and desperation.

"It's newer than my phone. I don't know how to mute it," he whispered.

Gina leaned close and examined it. "Me, neither."

Any second now, that phone was going to betray our location by blaring the Star Wars theme. I didn't know why, but Fred put the phone behind his back. The light dimmed to almost nothing and then went out. A dull clatter told me what he'd done. He'd forced it through one of the drafty spaces between the floor boards and one of the wall studs, dropping it down along the wall.

When it rang, the sound echoed eerily.

"Where's that coming from?" Mr. Collins shouted.

My directional sense wasn't the best, but I was pretty sure the phone ended up somewhere in the wall behind Gina's bed. They wouldn't be able to move a heavy piece of furniture like that without pulling the drawers out and taking the mattress off. The sounds that accompanied the dramatic orchestral notes from the cell phone told me they were doing just that. From the pounding thumps that followed, I guessed someone was kicking holes in the exposed wall.

"Here it is!"

The voices from below were much louder now.

"How'd they get it into the wall?"

Every muscle in my body was so tense waiting for them to sniff us out I felt I might shatter if someone said, "Boo."

"Who cares? Let's go. Take the notebook."

Gina made a little *eep* sound, like a mournful mouse.

We waited a long time after all the noises from below ceased before venturing out of our hidey-hole. Both my feet had fallen asleep, and when Fred lowered the ladder, they began to tingle unmercifully. I had to sit on a box. "I'll be down as soon as my feet come back to life."

"I hear you." Gina shook her leg but stumbled down the steps after Fred anyway, probably eager to see what was left of her bedroom. After maybe ten seconds, I heard a muffled scream and felt awful. Mr. Collins had taken her cats and her laptop and ripped holes in her wall, and it was all my fault. If I hadn't showed up, she'd be asleep with her cats curled around her feet by now. I was so wrapped up in self-recrimination I almost didn't catch on when Fred said loudly, "We're just bystanders, man."

Heart skipping beats, I tiptoed across the attic and peeked down into the hallway just in time to see Gina and Fred leave the bedroom, hands conspicuously in the air. Behind them, a man I'd never seen before gestured to the living room with the gun in his hand.

"We're going outside and you will very quietly and calmly get into my car or I will shoot you both in the head. Got it?" The man spoke in a no-nonsense voice that convinced me he meant it.

I didn't so much hear the front door open as feel the air pressure change, but before it slammed shut I was already digging through the box I'd overturned earlier. I grabbed a musty men's suit jacket and quickly descended the ladder. By the time I made it out the back door, Mr. Collins was buttoning the jacket across his narrow chest. I tripped over something buried in the snow, but made it around the side of the house before the man with the gun got settled in the driver's seat.

He turned as I strode up to him. He had his gun in his hand, but held it pointing downward. The street lamp was far enough away that I didn't see the surprise on his face. I did hear it in his tentative, "Sir?" though.

I feared the second I opened my mouth and spoke, he'd know what, if not exactly who, I was. My vocal range didn't go low enough to be taken for a man, nor had I ever managed to mimic a decent English accent. Of course, Mr. Collins wasn't much of a man, and the guy standing in front of me was American, so he'd be easier to fool than another Brit. I'd seen my teacher perform in front of class every day this past week; all I had to do was channel his abrasive personality.

Gina's pale, frightened face staring out through the back window at me was all the motivation I needed.

My shoulders went back and I tilted my head the way I'd seen Mr. Collins do. The lids of my eyes hovered at half-mast and I pursed my lips, moving forward a couple of steps with his signature goose-step.

"Ahem," I said.

"They were hiding in the attic the whole time," the man said, jerking his head at the car. I was gratified to hear the nervousness in his voice, although I found it hard to believe Mr. Collins could inspire it. Then it made sense when the man continued with, "I swear I checked every box and every corner."

"I need your gun," I said gruffly, holding out my hand.

The man raised his eyebrows but handed it to me, butt first, with no hesitation. "I thought you left with the others. You want a ride?"

I turned the gun around so the lethal end was pointing directly at his midsection. "You drive."

Chapter Thirty-one

I didn't want to shift in front of a witness, so I kept Mr. Collins' face, but spoke to Fred and Gina in my own voice.

"Guys? It's okay, it's me."

Fred laughed. "Awesome."

Gina got out of the car and said, "Be right back." She ran into her house.

I tried not to sound nervous as I ordered our captive put his hands on the roof of the car. Fred and I argued briefly about who was going to do what. I wanted him to go home, but he said, "I'm in this thing, Tainie."

Gina came back with a roll of duct tape. She brandished it front of our captive's face. "You like to break into people's houses and kidnap their kitties?" She tore off a piece of tape and slapped it over his mouth, patting it down firmly. "How do you like them apples?"

Fred was the voice of reason. "We should probably ask him where they're keeping Tainie's mother."

Gina was only too glad to rip the tape back off again. The man gave her a look that told her she'd better watch out if he got the upper hand. For someone being held at gunpoint, he didn't look appropriately cowed to me. It was probably patently obvious that just because I had his gun didn't mean I would use it. The truth was, I didn't even know how to use it. For all I knew the safety was on and this man was secretly playing us to learn more that he could use against us.

I stepped back and gestured to Fred to lean close. "Do you know how to use a gun?" He shook his head but Gina was standing close enough to have heard.

"Give it here." I passed her the gun. With her back to the man so he couldn't see her, she turned it on its side and twisted something.

"So, you remember I said my parents were zookeepers?" She spoke loud enough for the man to hear. "I've been on safari to Africa, walkabout in Australia and hiking across New Zealand. I am very familiar with how to use a pistol. This one has a full magazine and the safety is now off. I will not hesitate to put big round holes in anyone who vexes me."

I exchanged a grin with Fred, but our minor triumph was short-lived.

The man said, "Nice loud gunshot in this neighborhood? Cops'd be here in three minutes flat."

I stepped closer so I could look into his eyes. "Where's my mom?"

He looked me up and down insolently. "You know what Collins? I don't even know the lady."

"Oh, you're funny." Fred balled his hands into fists.

I put a hand on his arm. "It's alright. He doesn't know where she is. But the car does."

We left him lying on the floor of Gina's garage wrapped in a silver cocoon. After we got into the car, Gina said, "My mom is gonna be home at 6:30 in the morning. That's like four hours from now. We'd better figure out what to do with him before then because I do not want to be on the receiving end of her attitude if she finds him in the garage."

Fred drove while Gina rode shotgun so she could monitor the GPS. I changed back into Tory, but kept the old suit jacket on in case I needed to be Mr. Collins again.

"Turn left on Maple Avenue," said the robotic female GPS voice.

"How far is it?" I was getting nervous. We had no idea what we would find at our destination. For all I knew, we'd be greeted by an army of British agents with submachine guns and smiles.

"It says ten minutes," Gina said.

Fred glanced at the display. "Off Old Rathburn Road? There's a lot of private property out there, very isolated."

A good place for screams to go unnoticed.

"Turn left on First Street."

I looked out the rear window. When we'd first pulled away from the curb, I noticed headlights blink on from a car parked further down the block. The car began driving when we did and it might be a coincidence, but they made the same two turns as us, as well.

As we navigated the dark, nearly abandoned streets, we sank into silence; only the inhuman GPS voice occasionally broke it. The car behind us maintained its distance, but I was almost certain now it was following us. Houses thinned out, trees thickened and streetlights became few and far between.

"Turn right on Old Rathburn Road."

If our tail made this final turn I was going to tell Fred to do a quick u-turn and drive to the nearest police station. Thankfully, the car that had been following us since Gina's house kept going. After less than a hundred yards on Old Rathburn Highway, the GPS said, "You have reached your destination."

Fred slowed to a stop and dimmed the headlights, which did nothing to alleviate the spooky ambiance. Trees, trees and more trees surrounded us. There was no moon, but we were close enough to the city that the overcast sky reflected its light, leaving us not quite in pitch blackness. Patches of snow lining the road and among the vegetation seemed to glow.

"We're in the middle of nowhere," Gina said.

Fred pointed. "Nah, there's a driveway up ahead to the left. See the mailbox?

The last thing I wanted to do was go out there alone, but I told them, "Just drop me off here."

"What? Don't be stupid." Gina hefted the gun. "You need me."

"I need for you to be safe. If Fred's right and Penny got killed because of…people like me…"

"Shut up," Fred said.

"No! Listen." I found myself gripping the backs of their seats. "These guys kidnap people, right? And they neutralize witnesses. All I want to do is find out if Mom is here and then—then leave. If I don't come back within, say, an hour, I need to know someone will call the cops."

Fred patted my hand. "Well, it's not going to be me."

"Me, either." I could barely see Gina's smile in the dim light from outside. "Besides, I already brought the cops into it, sort of. I sent an email to the San Francisco police."

"To Zach Wong?" Fred asked. "He's kind of on the other side of the country."

Gina shrugged. "Covers two bases, though. If something happens to us, there's someone out there who knows. Plus, I told him the kidnappers wanted to talk to Caitlin. If he knows where she is, maybe she can come negotiate our release."

My mouth dropped open. "Do you hear yourself? I have no choice. I can't just sit around and wait for her to come rescue my mom, because it might never happen. But you're talking about risking your life, Gina."

"What life?" Gina almost shouted it, startling me. "We had a nice house and my parents made good money and I had friends who are all dead now! They only found half my dad's body! Now my mom works at McDonalds and I live in a crappy little house in an unfriendly town. You—you are the most exciting thing that has ever happened to me—including the Cataclysm. You are my only friend, and one thing you will learn about me, Titania, is that I'm loyal. To a fault."

I made the mistake of looking to Fred for support, but he just said,

"Let's go," and opened the door.

The driveway wasn't much more than a narrow dirt and gravel trail that had been grievously neglected. Fred discovered that our car benefactor kept a mini flashlight on his keychain. It didn't do much to cut the gloom, but it did show us where to step so we wouldn't fall into the deep potholes that riddled the trail.

I couldn't see anything up ahead; no lights indicating there was an inhabited structure. There were plenty of forest creatures that could see in the dark, though. I was too big to be a believable owl, but a wolf would work. Just as I was about to suggest to Fred and Gina that we stop so I could stash my clothes and shift, there was a sound from the underbrush behind us. Fred swung around with the little flashlight and I caught a glimpse of an animal bounding between the trees, paralleling the driveway.

Gina gasped. "Was that a deer?"

"Yeah," Fred said. "I told you this was the boonies."

What if something was chasing that deer? If I shifted into an animal that could see in the dark, what would happen if I encountered another animal, or worse, a predator? I wasn't exactly an animal behaviorist, but I did know that wolves in particular had social rules they followed. Still, the odds were probably slim there was another wolf, or a pack of wolves, haunting this neck of the woods. I'd be smarter to worry about armed goons, assuming there was an actual building at the end of this endless driveway. Goons with night vision scopes and no compunctions about shooting Bambi's mother, much less a dangerous-looking wolf.

"Guys, stop for a minute. What if I go in as a wolf?"

"Good idea, you could pretend you're our dog if we get caught."

Gina snorted. "And get tossed in cages like my kitties? I wonder how many other innocent fuzzies they've kidnapped."

"I'll be able to see in the dark, though."

Fred waved the flashlight around. "This is starting to fade."

"Yeah, but you won't be able to talk to us. I vote no."

"Well, since Gina has declared this to be a democracy," Fred said, "I vote yes. That's two to one."

I didn't need wolf-vision to see Gina's tongue make a brief appearance.

I stripped down as quickly as possible, realizing that in future I would have to learn to dress simply in easy-to-ditch clothes and lose the bulk of the modesty that made me want to hide my body even out here in cold, dark nowhere. Just before I shifted, I said, "One bark means yes, two means no."

We only got ten yards further before the deer we'd seen earlier leapt into the middle of the driveway and ran right for us. At first I thought the small doe was being chased by the goons I'd imagined earlier, but she stopped within the dim circle of light from Fred's flashlight.

"Uh…is this like a…deer in the headlights?" Gina tentatively raised the gun.

"Tainie's a wolf. Deer's probably scared literally stiff," Fred replied softly.

I am not a deer.

I looked up into the doe's huge brown eyes. In the faint light, they seemed to swirl.

I sent, *Who are you*?

Caitlin O'Connor. And you need to run. Now.

Chapter Thirty-two

I didn't ask any more questions; didn't need to. Caitlin's memory was clear in my mind: men in dark clothing were leaving a low brick building up ahead and climbing purposefully into a car. Since I couldn't very well tell Gina and Fred what was going on, I ran back to my clothes and shifted, snatching up my jacket and holding it in front of me as I rose to a standing position. As soon as my voice box formed, I said, "You guys—they're coming! Get back to the car!"

Gina paused to argue or ask questions, but when Caitlin the doe nudged her hard enough to make her pitch forward, she and Fred did as they were told. I hastily put on my jacket and boots, skipping the rest. Fred grabbed my hand as he ran past and pulled me along with him, but in doing so, he momentarily shifted the flashlight beam away from the ground in front of us. The regular rhythm of Gina's feet pounding the gravel stopped midstride and she went down with a grunt. We stopped to help her up, but as soon as she put weight on her right leg, she let out a cry of pain.

"Go!" I pushed Fred. "Move the car! We'll hide."

A set of headlights appeared from the direction we'd just come, all the encouragement he needed to take off again.

As we stumbled back to the place I'd stashed my clothes, Gina muttered, "I can't believe I'm the girl who falls when the monster is chasing her through the swamp."

The car was almost upon us when I realized there was no way Fred would make it in time. I tore off my jacket and kicked off my boots, shifting this time into a small deer, like Caitlin. I left Gina nursing her ankle behind a tree and trotted out on unfamiliar hooves. A second later, I was joined by Caitlin.

Lie down, she sent. *Play like you're hurt*.

It was exactly what I'd planned to do, the only thing I possibly could do. I bent my forelegs and fell awkwardly to my knees before rolling prone in the middle of the driveway. Caitlin stood over me in a protective stance, like I was her fawn. When the car reached us, the driver stopped. There wasn't enough room on the narrow track to go around. Dust and fog floated in front of the blinding headlights.

I rotated my large ears forward, my keen sense of hearing picking up the conversation inside the car. One of the passengers said, "Venison!"

Someone else said, "Put your damned gun away."

A man got out and walked towards us, waving his hands in the air, yelling, "Git! Move off, ya stupid deer!"

We ignored him until I picked up the faint sound of an engine firing to life. Fred had reached the car.

Caitlin sent, *He's safe. Let's go.*

I scrambled to my hooves and shot off into the trees, surprised at the power in my legs and my instinctive nimbleness. When the car had gone, I made my way back to Gina.

She was leaning on the tree, testing her ankle. "Is that you, Tainie?"

I forgot I couldn't talk and tried. Apparently, deer sound like chipmunks with kazoos stuck in their throats when they vocalize.

Gina jumped. "Don't do that!"

I shifted back into Tory and said, "Sorry."

I had to search for my boots, and my clothes were damp from melting snow, but I began dressing.

"Who's the other deer?" Gina asked. "And where'd it go?"

Before I could answer, a voice from out of the gloom said, "My name is Caitlin. Which one of you is Gina?"

"That would be me."

"Zach forwarded your email. It was somewhat garbled." Caitlin's speech was formal, with a faint Irish accent.

"Yeah, well, fear brings out the typos in me," Gina said.

Morning was several hours away, but the sky had lightened a bit. I couldn't see her face, but Caitlin had long, curly hair and wore a black cape. I suspected she was nude underneath.

She turned to me. "I do not know you, sister. Is this your true face?"

I shook my head. "I'm Tainie. I was on the ship, but we didn't meet. I accidently touched the crown the day you stopped the Cataclysm, but I swear I had no idea what would happen."

"It is fortunate you lived. I followed you here from Gina's house. I assume this is the place they are holding the others?"

I didn't know what Gina wrote in her email. "We aren't sure." As briefly as possible, I described my own kidnapping and the escape with Seamus, told her about the video Higgins sent us and the plan to rescue my mom, and finally, explained what happened at Gina's house. Caitlin didn't ask questions, but she probably didn't need to if she was reading my mind while I talked.

"Seamus would not be easy to catch a second time, but you are right that protecting your mother would make him vulnerable. I heard rumors that some of the folk who aided in stopping the Gossamer Sphere were disappearing, but none have been full Fae, like Seamus and I. From what you are telling me, they have already learned too much. This is dire news indeed. I am aggrieved to admit it is all a direct result of my own actions."

Caitlin's words and tone were full of self-recrimination, but at the moment I was neither sympathetic nor interested in hearing what she thought she'd done to set the agency employing Mr. Collins against us. I just wanted to find my mom.

Footsteps crunching on gravel told us someone was coming. I recognized Fred's silhouette.

"What'd I miss?" he asked.

I was instantly annoyed at the prospect of standing around talking some more; summing up recent events instead of doing something.

Still, Caitlin was here. She was the one who could fix everything, right?

Maybe she was still reading my mind, but she seemed to think it was time for action, too. She said, "The building beyond the lane is large and low, with several entrances, few windows, and a flat roof. There are cameras at each corner of the structure, so I think it best that we approach from the sky. Have you flown?"

"Only in an airplane." I hadn't had time to give it a lot of thought, but the idea of becoming a bird and flying through the open sky scared me almost as much as being in the water.

"Hm. No time for lessons now. There's no ground cover except at the back of the building. Have you been a snake?"

I shuddered at the very thought. "I've been a dog and an otter. Oh, and a deer."

"You've had months to practice and that's all you've attempted?"

"I—I didn't know I was a—a shapeshifter until a few days ago."

"I see. Well, a snake is really the only option to get you past the cameras if you can't fly. The only problem with becoming a snake is their brains are very different from that of mammals. It rather muddles the thought processes and I think you are too inexperienced for that."

I nodded rapidly up and down to indicate sincere agreement.

"It's too cold for a reptile anyway. Best I go in alone," Caitlin said. "You three wait here. Stay off the lane so you can hide quickly."

"Caitlin?" I asked.

"Yes."

"I probably should have mentioned something. Seamus, and my mom, too, for that matter, suspected all of this was a ruse to draw you out of hiding."

"Well, then. They've succeeded, haven't they?"

Chapter Thirty-three

Caitlin dropped the cape and shifted into something long and lean and low. In the poor light, I wasn't sure what she became, but it wasn't a bird. She ran to the nearest tree and leapt up, climbing and clawing her way up until I lost sight of her.

"Was that a jaguar?" Fred asked quietly.

It made sense when I thought about it. "She'll be a big bird, so she'll need height to take wing among these trees."

The three of us peered up into the branches. After a few minutes, a large black shadow swept across the sky.

"She's off!" Gina said, like she was commentating a race. I wondered if she took anything seriously.

Time seemed to stop as we waited. Beneath the constant worry, I became conscious of how cold, tired and hungry I was. We sat at the edge of the driveway on a dry patch of ground, close enough that we could dive behind the nearest tree and hide if need be. I felt horrible about staying behind. Cowardly even. What was the use of having such an incredible gift if I was too frightened to use it? On the other hand, Caitlin herself had nixed my participation. The last thing she'd need was an amateur slowing her down. Probably, hopefully, she was inside that intimidating building right now, kicking some bad-guy butt and saving my mom.

Inside the pockets of the jacket I'd found in Gina's attic, I crossed my fingers.

I'm not sure how much time passed. Gina leaned against me and somehow, despite the discomfort of sitting on cold, rocky ground, dozed off. Fred sat on the other side with his arm around me. I appreciated his warmth and tried not to think about his closeness. I wanted to talk to him about so many things, but circumstances being what they were, it just wasn't the right time.

The sound of tires on gravel startled us all. The vehicle that had left earlier was returning, accompanied by two other cars and the white van.

My limbs were stiff and I must have been in a pre-sleep state, because I was slow to react. Fred, too, seemed groggy and disoriented. Gina actually responded more quickly than us, maybe because suddenly waking from sleep comes along with a shot of adrenaline. She scrambled on her hands and knees behind the nearest tree. Fred and I followed, barely ducking down in time to avoid the sweep of headlights as the lead car rounded a bend.

"What about Caitlin?" Gina whispered.

"We have no way to warn her."

The cars went past us. I was wide awake now, frustrated and more scared than ever. If I waited and did nothing, Caitlin would soon be outnumbered. Not that I had any idea how many people were already inside. And quite a bit of time had passed; for all I knew, she'd been caught and locked up some time ago.

At that moment, all I knew for certain was that I couldn't continue to sit by and do nothing.

I said, "Wait here, guys."

I only took one step before Fred grabbed both my arms and stopped me.

"What are you doing?" he asked.

"Getting a closer look."

"I'm coming, too."

I knew better than to argue. Gina didn't say anything for once and at first I thought she was going to wait this one out. Then I saw her remove the gun from her pocket and twist the safety. Fred had to support her as she limped along.

It was still a few hours from dawn, but the sky was much lighter. We stayed near the edge of the driveway, but off the gravel so the noise wouldn't give us away. When we got close enough to see and hear the men as they exited the cars, we stopped and stayed out of sight behind some scrub brush and young trees.

I had barely settled in to watch when one of the men opened the back door of his car and pulled someone out. Fred quickly placed his hand over my mouth, which was a good thing, because as soon as I saw my mom, bound at the wrists and gagged, I almost shouted out.

Once the man shoved her ahead of him into the building, the remaining men, four of them, gathered at the back of the sedan. They all had what looked like large guns, but with some kind of yellow markings.

"Tasers," Fred whispered.

The tallest of the men said, "Ready?" and must have pressed a button on his keychain, because the trunk popped open. Whatever or whoever was inside wasn't moving, but the men didn't relax. Two stood back while the others holstered their weapons and reached inside.

It took some effort for them to haul the limp occupant out of the trunk. They got him partially clear of the edge and then just let him roll out and fall to the ground. He landed with a thump on his side, but remained unresponsive, pale face turned in our direction.

Next to me, I heard Gina murmur, "What the hell?"

"It's Seamus," I said. He was still wearing Fred's likeness.

Even though he appeared to be unconscious, I tried to contact him. To my surprise, his eyes opened. The men around him all stepped back. The two who'd holstered their weapons pulled them back out again.

"Don't try anything funny," the tallest one said in a Cockney accent. "Or it's shocky-shocky for you."

Seamus, can you hear me?

Yes.

Caitlin is here! She's in the building.

That's very bad news. You must get away from here.

I saw them take Mom inside. What's plan B?

As it happens, I'm fresh out of ideas.

"On your feet, freak." The tall man kicked Seamus in the back.

I pulled off my boots and sent, *I'll distract them. You roll under the car.*

He tried to respond, but I broke eye contact to remove my shirt. Fred politely turned away, but I took his head in my hands and made him look into my eyes.

"Take Gina home. Promise me."

I read his mind; knew he was stubbornly determined to stay. I didn't have time to argue, so I stepped back and shifted. A deer wouldn't get the kind of reaction I wanted, so I took a page out of Caitlin's book and chose something a little more deadly.

I needed the element of surprise; not only did I leap out into the middle of the driveway, but I let out a growling scream. The men turned to gape at the sudden appearance of a charging mountain lion. All four of them raised their Tasers at me, but only two fired. I jumped to the left and their shots missed. The third man fired and his shot was way off the mark. The tall man seemed to be waiting for me to get closer—he had a bead on me—but Seamus hadn't rolled under the car.

An angry black bear ripped the Taser out of the tall man's hand and knocked him to the ground. I leapt over him and landed all-claws-out on the chest of the man on Seamus' other side. He went down under my weight with a cry of pain and tried to bring his spent Taser into play, but I raked him with all four sets of claws as I sprang away. I saw the first two men turn their reloaded weapons on us and thought the game was over.

"Hey, morons!" Fred shouted. Everyone turned to look. He was standing just out of Taser reach. "I'm getting away!" He began running down the driveway, toward where Gina was hiding. The two uninjured men chased after him. As soon as Fred disappeared into the woods where Gina was waiting, they stopped dead in their tracks and raised their arms in surrender. From here, I couldn't see her, but I knew Gina's real gun trumped their electric ones.

I shifted back into Tory, picked up the tall man's Taser and shot the man I'd raked with my claws. He stiffened up and appeared to go into a seizure. Seamus shifted into the tall man's face and form and then punched him in the face, knocking him out cold. Immediately, he began removing the man's pants.

"Stay down, so the cameras can't see you," he said.

I was already shielded by the still-open trunk lid, but I ducked down further. The man I shot pulled the Taser wires from his chest and seemed about to try something, so I pointed the tall man's Taser at him and he froze.

"Strip," I ordered.

Between us, Seamus and I stripped the men, stashed their bodies, one unconscious and one barely cooperative, in the trunk and dressed in their bloody clothes all in the space of a few minutes. I, too, shifted and became a much-thinner version of the man I'd zapped. His clothes were way too big for me, but I cinched his belt to the innermost hole and hoped no one would notice.

If anyone was monitoring the cameras, they didn't respond to the chaos by confronting us outside.

"Let's go," Seamus said. I hefted my Taser and followed him to the building. The door must have been a side entrance because inside was a long corridor, lit by two bare bulbs mounted along the right side. The air was overly warm and humid. Panels in the suspended ceiling were marred with water stains. The floor was bare concrete and the walls had been painted yellow at some point, but were now dull and dirty. Six doors with narrow reinforced windows in them lined the corridor, three on each side across from each other. Seamus took the right while I took the left. All of the windows were dark, but we tried each locked door before approaching a cross-corridor.

More doors. He pointed to an interior security camera. I suppressed the urge to wave at it. If anyone was watching, they knew we were here. The question was: did they know we weren't who we appeared to be? An astute observer would notice that we didn't seem to know our way around. At best they'd be suspicious, at worst they'd be waiting.

"What is this place?" I asked.

Seamus gestured to some faded words stenciled on one of the doors that read 'Isolation Room.'

"Looks like an old insane asylum or jail."

"Appropriate ambiance," I said. "Which way?"

He took a deep breath and closed his eyes, letting the air out slowly. When he opened them, his gaze went back to the Isolation Room. It was the only door without a little window.

I raised the Taser gun in a suddenly shaking hand and pressed myself against the wall as he turned the knob and opened the door a crack. A strip of light brightened the rough cement floor and oddly, the scent of popcorn floated out. Before we could make our move, someone inside said, "Come in already!" With deep dread, I recognized Mr. Collins' voice.

The room was bigger than it looked from the outside. Equipment was set up everywhere and one whole wall was covered with monitors, much like the room Higgins had occupied at the place they'd held us, but on a larger scale. A man with his back to us typed on a keyboard, but my attention was all for Mr. Collins, who leaned against a counter with a microwave on it. He held out a bag of popcorn and asked, "Want some?"

"Where's my mom?"

I pointed the Taser at him, but he seemed not to notice. He produced an exaggerated frown and dug around in his bag. "Ask Higgs."

Shocked, I looked at the other man. Higgins spun his office chair around and gave us a cheerful smile. "Hey, Tainie. Seamus. Like how this all worked out? You alien freaks can read minds, but I still fooled you."

"That's because we're human," I said between gritted teeth. "We make mistakes."

He laughed. "If you're human, I'm Tom Cruise. Well, I'm a better actor anyway. You want to see your mom?" He reached around and tapped a few keys. A new view appeared on the largest monitor and I caught my breath. It was a close-up of my mom, still gagged. Someone off-camera gripped her by the hair, pulling her head back while his other hand pressed a knife to her throat. Tears leaked out of her frightened eyes and a drop of blood trailed down to pool along her clavicle.

"Great resolution, huh?" Higgins said. "Look how red that blood is."

His joviality was so offensive I was speechless.

Seamus wasn't. His voice was low. "Let her go. She isn't one of us."

Mr. Collins stepped towards us, exploring his teeth with his tongue for stray bits of popcorn. "Read my mind: she's dead if you don't tell us where to find Caitlin O'Connor."

He returned Seamus' probing stare with a sneer on his face. "That's right, we've got orders not to kill anyone, but they wouldn't have hired me if they wanted someone who blindly followed orders."

"You're monologuing, Collins," Higgins sang out.

"So? Anything I know, they know. Why do you think we've been kept in the dark about so much of this op? So we seemed sincere; so they didn't learn anything from us that would tip them off."

"What do you want?" I asked.

Mr. Collins made a *tsk-tsk* noise and said, "As if you didn't know."

He and Higgins were infuriatingly confident. They had us where they wanted us and weren't too shy to gloat. Neither of them happened to be looking at the monitor, however, so they didn't see what Seamus and I saw.

"All we want is a certain crown." Mr. Collins affected a bored tone. "Give us that and you're all free to go."

"We don't have to read your mind to know that's untrue," I said, trying not to let my eyes stray to the monitor and give anything away.

He shrugged and opened his mouth to spew some more despicable lies, but Seamus sent, *Now*! and without hesitation I fired the Taser at Higgins' midsection. At the same time, with a smooth and seemingly effortless motion, Seamus kicked Mr. Collins in the face, snapping his head back. Before the shocked man could recover his equilibrium, he found himself face down on the filthy cement floor with Seamus' knee in his back.

I looked back at the monitor, where previously we'd seen flashes of a big cat, probably a leopard, attack whoever had been holding my mom. Now the body of a man in his underwear lay bent and twisted against the far wall, and closer inspection showed it to be the same guy we'd left taped up in Gina's garage. At first I thought he was dead, but the resolution really *was* good; I saw his chest rise and fall. Neither Mom nor Caitlin was in the room.

Higgins, who was still miraculously sitting upright in the chair, moaned. Drool dribbled out of the corner of his slack mouth. I barely suppressed the urge to slap him.

"You won't get away!" Mr. Collins couldn't quite achieve a yell with the weight of a full-grown man on his back. Seamus grasped a handful of his hair and pulled his head back, just like my mom's captor had done.

I went over and knelt down in front of him. Time to clear a few things up.

"Did you kill Penny Wharton?"

Too late, he tried to look away, his contorted face turning beet red. He ignored my question, but I already had my answer.

"We know everything about you!" he spat. "Right now an army of agents is headed this way and they will wipe your vile species from the planet!"

"Liar," I said mildly. I stood and turned away from him in disgust. I didn't see what Seamus did, but I heard a sickening thump and knew he'd cracked Mr. Collins' head against the cement. The casual violence made my stomach lurch. I put a hand to my mouth.

Seamus straightened up and glanced at me. "They have already done far worse to us."

I knew it, knew objectively that mercy shown now would only leave them free to come back against us later, but I said, "Don't kill them."

He gave me a startled look. "I never kill unless I have to. He'll be fine." Then he pointed. "Look."

One of the monitors showed my mom and Caitlin leaving the building.

While he took a moment to tie Higgins to the chair with the Taser wires, I grabbed the small purple notebook I'd seen sitting on the counter next to the microwave. Then we went back down the corridor and out the door. It seemed to me that it should be morning by now, but it wasn't quite.

Caitlin, wearing a man's clothing, stood near the trees with my mom, Fred, and Gina. The two men Gina had been holding at gunpoint were nowhere to be seen.

"Mom!" I shouted and ran toward her. She gave me a strange look, and I realized I was still wearing the guise of the man in the trunk. By the time I reached her, I had shifted into myself. We threw our arms around each other.

She gripped my face, hurting my cheeks. "Are you alright?"

"I'm fine."

We clutched each other close and she buried her face in my hair. After a few seconds, I pulled away and wiped my eyes, conscious that we still needed to put some acreage between us and this place.

"We'll take one of these cars and drive it to mine," Caitlin said, nodding to the sedans.

Seamus went to the car next to the one where we'd stashed the men in the trunk, but both Fred and Gina said, "Not that one!"

Seamus frowned. "Why not?"

A pounding from inside the trunk told us where the other two men had gone.

"Is there a vehicle we can use that doesn't have bad guys in the trunk?" Seamus asked with a twist of the lips that might have been a smile in a different situation.

The third car over had no bad guys, but it did have a surprise inside.

Gina took one look in the back seat and exclaimed, "Queenie! Fred!" Her cats were sleeping unharmed in a wire crate.

"Oh, and here." I held out her notebook.

"Yay, a happy ending," she said.

"Let us get fully away before congratulating ourselves," Caitlin said.

We all squeezed in, sitting on top of one another because the cat crate took up half the back seat. Seamus gestured to the steering wheel. "No keys."

Caitlin reached over, put her hand on the steering column and the engine roared to life.

Seamus raised his eyebrows. "I didn't know we could do that."

"We are all electrical beings," Caitlin said as he backed down the driveway. "The Folk merely have the means to use our natural electrical forces in unique ways. How do you think we access the thoughts of others?"

"Same old Caitlin. Always spoiling the magic by lecturing on the science. Never mind the lesson. I arrived in the trunk of a car. I need directions."

Chapter Thirty-four

Caitlin's car was a rental, but fortunately she'd opted for a good-sized SUV rather than an economy car, so it held us all comfortably. Gina sat in the rear-most seat with her disgruntled kitties next to her. I sat in the middle seat with Fred on one side and Mom on the other. I kept my own face to appease my mom, but averted it from Fred so wouldn't remember me this way.

Even though they had to be as exhausted in body and mind as I was, Gina and Fred bombarded us with questions, which we answered as best we could.

"I still don't get it," Fred said, after Seamus revealed what he'd learned from Mr. Collins. "Why the elaborate set-up?"

Caitlin answered. "They needed to ensure that someone on the outside knew about the kidnappings. Someone who potentially had access to me. That's why they let Seamus escape the first time. They held him long enough to convince him the Folk were all in dire danger."

"It was always to get us to reveal Caitlin's whereabouts," Seamus replied. "They had orders not to harm us, but they needed us to believe they would. The agents didn't know all the facts of the op. Even Collins and Higgins were kept in the dark about key factors, like the locator in Higgins' cell phone. I'm guessing both were chosen because they are convincing liars. I didn't bother to read Higgins when he said he was on our side; a mistake I will not make again."

"So why did Higgins send us those names?" Fred asked.

I answered. "To help us find Caitlin in case we didn't know where she was."

Gina poked her fingers between the bars of the crate to comfort her meowing cats. "So, does a person really have to be descended from the Folk or whatever to become a shapeshifter? How does that work?"

Caitlin's face in the rear-view mirror was grave. "That is precisely the question these men would like to answer. Do you understand why they might want to know how to turn an ordinary person into something such as I? The covert military implications alone boggle one's mind, especially given the fact that the 'technology' would be impossible to contain within a single country."

Gina nodded. "Trust would go down the toilet; make the cold war look like a game of Stratego."

Caitlin laughed. She had a beautiful laugh to go along with the face I could finally see clearly. "The world has yet to recover from what the Gossamer Sphere has done to it. If I told you why the Cataclysm occurred, you would be more astounded than you were when Titania first showed you what we are. And if the gossamer crown were to fall into the hands of men such as those who've gone to these great lengths to obtain it, do you think the world would ever recover?"

Gina shook her head solemnly. "Are you guys going to disappear now?" She looked at me, but I dropped my eyes. In my lap, my hands were clasped around my mother's hand.

Caitlin stopped the car. We were at the mall.

"We are grateful for your help," she said. "Without your courage, it is doubtful we would be free. However, times being what they are, the Folk must hide more deeply than ever, not only to protect themselves, but to protect…everyone. Titania no longer exists. Her shadow will always be on the run, and those who shelter in it will always inherit the danger."

She was talking to Gina, but her message was for me.

"Fred, please drive Gina home in this car and let the rental company know where to find it. Titania, say goodbye to your friends—quickly."

As soon as Caitlin, Seamus and Mom got out of the car, I became Tory and finally turned to Fred. It took all my willpower to keep myself from crying.

Gina let out a gigantic sigh and asked, "Was last night for real, or did we all eat some bad mushrooms?"

I smiled. "If I had a choice, I'd pick the shrooms."

Fred took my hand. I didn't expect him to with Gina right there, but he leaned over and gave me a sweet, lingering kiss. "I want to tell you how I feel about you, but…I'm pretty mixed up inside. I wish you didn't have to go."

That broke the dam. The tears I was holding back spilled over. There was no point confessing all that was in my heart. He was my first kiss, my first love, my first everything.

I tried to memorize the exact color of his blue eyes, the shape of his lips. "Maybe someday people like me won't have to hide."

Gina sighed loudly. "Maybe someday there'll only be peace and love in the world, and innocent people won't have to die."

It would be great to ignore her and stretch the moment with Fred, but her comment reminded me of something. I felt my smile fade away. I gave Fred's hand a little tug.

"I found out who killed Penny."

He looked relieved, heartened. "Who?"

I'd seen it in Mr. Collins' mind. He'd been watching Penny's house. They'd traced the email Mom sent to Seamus, the one asking what to do about me. She'd had to borrow Mrs. Wharton's computer, had used Penny's email account—that's how they found us. Mr. Collins saw Stephen and Fred drop Penny off just like Fred told me. But after Penny's argument with her mother, she stormed out and called Stephen on her cell.

"It was an accident," I said. "She slipped and started to fall into the pool. He grabbed for her, but caught her around the neck."

Fred was wary now. "Who? Tell me."

Mr. Collins had seen it when Stephen lost his grip and dropped her into the pool; saw him go in after her and try to revive her. Then, instead of calling anyone for help, he ran, leaving his car parked on the street.

"Stephen asked you to go back for his car, didn't he?"

Fred blanched. "Oh, God."

"I know you saw her in the pool, Fred. Why didn't you call 911?" There were plenty of places that no longer had emergency services since the Cataclysm, but Philadelphia wasn't one of them.

What I really wanted to know was how he could look me in the eye the other day and tell me Stephen didn't do it. How, despite the evidence, he could truly believe such a thing.

He shook his head, tiny movements of denial. "After we dropped her off, I went to bed. Then later, Stephen woke me up and said he'd gone back, said they'd partied, he got drunk and walked home and didn't want to get busted when Grampa saw the car was gone. So, yeah, I did go get it. But I never saw Penny in the pool."

I hadn't been reading him, but now I did—and found he was telling the truth. Yet once again I saw the image in his mind, that of Penny's face under water in the pool. But then I realized Fred's image showed clear water, when the water at the bottom of the pool had been thick with green algae. And Fred's version of Penny had her eyes closed and her expression was peaceful instead of horrified.

It hadn't been a memory at all. As disturbed as I was at the concept that a vivid imagination could fool me, I was also tremendously relieved.

Fred, however, was devastated.

"He told me he had nothing to do with it," he said softly.

"It was an accident," I said.

A knock on the window told us our time was up. I wanted to console him, wanted to kick Gina and her cats out of the car and drive far away where Fred and I could be alone.

Gina said, "Quick, before the poetic princess makes you get out—how can we get hold of you?"

I shook my head, fresh tears starting at the answer. "You can't."

"Okay, fine, be that way. But I'm on Facebook and I friend just about everyone but spammers, so if you change your mind or get lonely on the run, make up a fake username and gimme a poke. Use the secret word 'niacin' and I'll know it's you."

"I might just do that…promise me something, you guys?"

They waited.

"Promise you'll stay friends."

Fred's lips twisted in a subdued version of that crooked grin I loved so well. "Who else are we going to talk to about the bad mushrooms we ate last night?"

Epilogue

Money is magic.

And Caitlin had loads of it. I guess being two thousand years old taught her a thing or two about finances. After we bought new clothes at the mall, we took a cab all the way to New York. Seamus said his goodbyes and disappeared—just like that.

I thought Caitlin would do the same and Mom and me would be on our own. Instead, Caitlin hooked us up with fake identification and gave us some money. A lot of money.

She said it was because my mom needed to go back to school, become something one hundred percent removed from nursing. She suggested Mom lose the extra weight, adopt a more classic style instead of the wild, bright get-ups, and have her hair professionally cut.

I, of course, didn't need a disguise. I didn't look like Tory anymore, but I was just as pretty. I simply repaired all of my defects: lengthened my bones, redistributed my fat stores, lifted my hairline, enlarged my eyes, refined my skin, adopted Mom's nose and set my lower jaw into its proper place. I was the new, improved Tainie. No fairy-godmother-supplied major reconstructive surgery necessary.

That wasn't my name anymore, though. I was ambivalent about my new identity: Julie Jones. Mom got the better name, Hannah, but I wasn't in any position to complain. At least we were safe.

Caitlin also helped us clean up in our wake: she got a message to my school that I was leaving, and another one to Gramma Foster so she wouldn't report us to the police as missing persons.

And that was that. Kind of depressing that no one, aside from Fred, Gina and maybe Tamika, would even notice I was gone.

Once we were settled in a nice apartment, Caitlin disappeared. She didn't say goodbye and didn't leave a forwarding address. I suspected, given the fact that I was doomed—or blessed—depending on how you looked at it, to live a long life, that I would see her again someday.

At my new school, I made friends more easily than I ever had before. It had been two months and my best friend was a thin, energetic junior varsity cheerleader named Miriam. Her large family was a noisy presence in our apartment complex. Her parents had been refugees from Somalia before becoming refugees from Texas. I met her because I was trying to be the opposite of Tainie. I didn't have the chops to be a cheerleader myself, but the coach needed an assistant, and my organizational skills fit the bill. That's how I discovered not all cheerleaders were stuck-up sadists like Jessica.

Because so few public schools could afford to offer sports anymore, our basketball team participated in a newly-formed interstate scholastic sports league. Our second away game was against Ashworth Academy. The cheerleaders, and me, were attending.

I hate to admit I didn't tell Mom exactly where I'd be, but she'd gotten into the bad habit of smothering me with motherly concern. We'd already verified that Mr. Collins was no longer a teacher there. Caitlin believed that agents had been specifically placed in all Philadelphia area schools just to locate me. The British covert intelligence agency responsible had interrogated the crew of the scientific ship we'd been on to identify the passengers. Mom recalled telling the ship's captain we were from the Philly area.

It was a rainy spring day. Miriam had no idea why I was in such a pensive mood, but she and the other cheerleaders were busy discussing their routine on the bus, so she gave me my space. The first glimpse I got of Fred was when he ran onto the court with the team. He was tall and muscular and I saw more than one of our own cheerleaders check him out. Typical Fred; he didn't so much ignore them as not realize he was stirring up so much interest. He didn't seem the same to me, though. His smile was not so quick to make an appearance.

That was probably due to his brother's incarceration. Stephen had pleaded guilty to involuntary manslaughter, which confused me since I knew it had been an accident. Maybe it had more to do with what the jury would think, what they'd make of his actions when he fled the scene instead of calling for help. Either way, the tragedy seemed to have affected Fred, made him grow up in hurry.

Within minutes of the first quarter of the game, it became clear that Ashworth Academy had a better team. Fred and his friend Barkley, whose jersey now read 'Voorhees,' because I'd been such a dunce I didn't realize the shirt he'd been wearing when I first identified him bore the name of his hero, basketball great Charles Barkley, dominated the play. I sat in the row behind our cheerleaders, among a group of Ashworth students who'd been forced to sit on the opposing team's side because of the huge turnout.

After about ten minutes, I became aware that someone had come to sit next to me. She had a little purple notebook on her lap and was typing away, seemingly oblivious to the game. Her wispy hair was held back with a brown lace headband and her skin looked clear, like she'd found an acne regimen that worked.

"Did you know," she said out of the blue, "that vitamin B3 lowers cholesterol?"

I smiled. "You mean niacin?"

She raised her eyes from the notebook and studied my face. "I see what you did. It's subtle, but you're still recognizable."

"Really?" I looked out on the court, saw Fred standing by the bench, wiping his sweaty face with a towel.

"Oh, yeah," Gina said. "He'll know it's you the second he sees you."

And then he saw me.

The end

www.ingramcontent.com/pod-product-compliance
Lightning Source LLC
Chambersburg PA
CBHW061238170626
46809CB00007B/2734

* 9 7 8 1 9 5 4 3 5 2 1 4 8 *